Death Fricassee

RECIPE FOR DEATH - BOOK 1

ISBN 978-1-68230-251-4

Formatting by Champagne Formats

TAWDRA KANDLE

Champagne
Formats

Other Books by the Author

The King Series
Fearless
Breathless
Restless
Endless

The Posse

The Perfect Dish Duo
Best Served Cold
Just Desserts

The Serendipity Duet
Undeniable
Unquenchable

The One Trilogy
The Last One

Prologue

Lucas

AWARENESS, WHEN IT pounced on me, was swift and brutal.

I groaned. My tongue felt like sandpaper, and the tip of it was stuck to the roof of my mouth. *When. . .and why. . .had I eaten a bundle of copper wire. . .from the bottom of a garbage can?* My mouth tasted like shit, with a subtle metallic undertone.

I rolled over, which wasn't as easy as it sounds since every muscle of my body, large and small, felt like it was on fire. The sheet around my hips slid down, and a cool draft of air hit me where it shouldn't have. *Why the hell was I naked?* My eyes flew open, and I leaped off the bed, my gaze darting around the room. Waking up nude only happened when I was in bed with a woman, and there wasn't one of those in sight.

I grabbed my head, moaning at the stabbing pain between my eyes. I sank to the edge of the bed and then fell back, hissing, when the sunlight that filtered through the heavy hotel room curtains hit me. The brightness intensified the pounding in my head.

Nausea gripped me. *Hangover.* Maybe the worst one I'd ever had. Christ almighty, what'd happened last night?

Memory began to return. A farewell party, thrown by some of the faculty of the college I was leaving as well as some of my former students, now proud college grads. We'd met at the local bar in town, the plan being to toss back a few beers, have some laughs and say good-bye before I took off for my new life in Florida. But somehow after four or five beers, staying to enjoy the local band had become more appealing. We'd done shots, and other people had joined us.

I'd turned to speak to a friend, and that's when I'd seen her. She stood at the bar between two stools, both of which were occupied by guys who were checking her out. She didn't even acknowledge them. Dark hair waved around her shoulders and her lithe body screamed to be touched, but it was her eyes that haunted me with their familiarity. When she turned that startling blue gaze on me, I nearly stuttered, because she reminded me of Cathryn, my ex-girlfriend. Or rather, the girl I'd hoped would be mine, until she'd broken up with me two weeks before. This woman's eyes were the same, yes, but there was more. She was taller than Cathryn, and her hair was shiny black instead of white-blonde. But they both had the simmer just beneath the cool exterior, an occasional flash of molten lava under a layer of rock.

I didn't remember anything after I'd begun talking to the woman. The rest of the night was a blank, as though I'd traveled in time from the moment we'd met to the second I'd opened my eyes just now. Maybe I had. I'd learned from Cathryn that there was more to the world than most of us guessed, much more than what we saw on the surface.

At least I knew where I was, even if I didn't recall how I'd gotten back here last night. I'd checked into the hotel just before meeting my friends. There was a few days' gap between the end of my lease on the townhouse just off campus and my scheduled

2

departure to the Sunshine State, so I'd decided to hang out at the local Holiday Inn while I tied up a few loose ends.

I was pretty certain I wouldn't be doing anything today except groaning in bed, and maybe worshipping at the porcelain throne. At least I'd be doing it at a hotel, where I could lay around in peace and not have to clean up after myself. My stomach turned over again, and I sprinted for the bathroom, barely making it before retching over the toilet bowl.

I collapsed back against the cool tile wall, breathing hard. God, I was too old for this shit. I hadn't gotten that wasted in years—I remembered doing shots last night, but I didn't think I'd done enough to make me feel this bad. I frowned, wondering if this were something else. Food poisoning, maybe? Or death eating me from the inside out?

I pushed myself up, and as I did, a flutter of white paper caught my eye. It was taped to the bathroom mirror, blowing a little in the rush of air from the vent in the ceiling. I reached for it with hands that still shook from my vomit session.

The writing was slanted, neat curlicues that made me think of the copy of the Declaration of Independence I'd seen in Philadelphia on school trips. Or maybe on the wedding invitations from all my friends who'd gotten married over the years. None of my students submitted anything that wasn't computer-generated these days, and it was weird to see handwriting.

Lucas,

I realize you're awaking with many questions, and quite likely feeling rather ill. I apologize that I couldn't linger to be more help to you, but my hasty departure was unavoidable.

I have, however, set up a delivery for you. The messenger should be arriving before noon, at which time I hope you're up and able to receive what you need. Follow your instincts, my friend.

I'll try to be in touch with you as soon as possible, but until then, trust that I did what was necessary, and try to forgive me.

3

Fate is a tricky thing. Yours has been set for years, and I'm not yet certain whether my own actions have circumvented it or complicated it. Time will tell.

Veronica

P.S. I'd be remiss if I didn't thank you for an enjoyable evening prior to our business. Your enthusiasm is matched only by your endowment. Our time together brought me more pleasure than I'd anticipated. Until next time.

I read it once, twice and then let the paper fall to the counter. None of the words made any sense, beyond her observation that I was probably waking up with questions. And vomiting. She hit the bulls-eye there.

But what kind of delivery had she arranged? Drugs? Had this chick dosed me with something? I'd read a book once where an enemy agent had seduced a regular guy, injected him with a toxic cocktail and then used the promise of an antidote to black-mail the dude into going on missions for her. Was Veronica an undercover spy? And just what did she expect from me?

I scanned my arms for any signs of needle marks, but there were none I could see. I twisted in front the mirror, checking out my ass. I didn't see tracks, but maybe she'd used one of those super-fine needles. Who knew what secret agents were capable of doing?

And what was all the fate shit in the note? She'd circum-vented or complicated what? Was I supposed to be killed last night, and she'd saved me? I raked my hand through my hair, making it stand on end. Leaning in closer to the sink, I studied my face in the mirror. Did I look different? Paler? I narrowed my eyes. Nah, that was probably just side effects of my hangover. I hoped. But my eyes. . .I opened them wide now. Instead of the blue I'd looked out through my whole life, they were now brown. What the hell had happened to my eyes?

The rest of my body felt okay. It was in the same condition I'd been maintaining for a long time. Not too bad for a guy pushing forty, I thought. And hey, apparently I'd impressed the mystery woman who may or may not have tried to kill me, both with my endurance and endowment. That was something. I glanced down at the note again and realized she hadn't written 'endurance', she'd said 'enthusiasm'. Well, I'd just focus on the endowment part.

A pounding at the door made me jump. I staggered out of the bathroom, and finding a pair of basketball shorts hanging out of my duffel bag, pulled them on. Another fist on the door was accompanied by a voice.

"Hey! Delivery for Mr. Reilly here."

I cleared my throat. "Yeah, hold on. I'm coming." I turned a T-shirt right side out and stretched it over my head. Before I opened the door, I put one eye to the peephole.

The guy who stood on the other side was probably older than me by about ten years. He was balding, with a paunch and a bored expression. The muscle shirt he wore had seen better days; the slogan across the front—*Trust Shorty*—was barely readable. He held a cooler in one hand.

I unlocked the door, and sliding back the chain, cracked it open. "Hey. Sorry. I was. . ." I cleared my throat. "Sleeping."

He smirked, his eyes raking up and down my body. "Yeah." He thrust the white and red cooler toward me along with a printed form. "Here ya go. It's pre-paid, so you're good to go. Sign on the bottom line. Lady said to tell you to look for the note."

I braced one hand on the door jam. "Yeah, I got it. What lady? What'd she look like?" I wanted to grab this guy by the collar of his grimy shirt and shake answers out of him.

He held up the hand not holding the cooler and stepped back. "I got no idea. I just make the deliveries. I know nothing." His beady black eyes met mine, and abruptly, I was dizzy, as numbers floated in front of my mind.

Five years, six months, three days. Five years, six months, three days.

5

It repeated, the words ringing in my ears and blinking into my field of vision. I stumbled back into the room, just catching the edge of the door before it swung shut. "What is that? What does it mean?"

"Buddy, what're you talking about?" Shorty glanced behind him, up and down the empty corridor of the hotel. "I didn't hear nothing. Or see nothing, either. You sick or something?" He dropped the cooler on the floor and backed up further, his forehead wrinkled and his mouth tight.

Five years, six months, three days. Five years, six months, three days

"What the hell is going on?" I was almost begging him now.

"I'm telling you, I don't know. Some dame came by, paid ahead and set up a delivery schedule. We don't ask questions, we just do our jobs."

"This woman—did she have black hair? And really bright blue eyes?"

Shorty shrugged. "I dunno, man. I didn't see her. She talked to the front office, and I'm just the delivery guy, right?" He must've decided I wasn't too great a threat, since he took a tentative step forward. "You don't mind me saying it, you don't look so hot. Want me to call you a doctor or something? Tell the front desk to send you someone?"

I shook my head. "No. I'm okay." I just needed to lie down and get these screaming numbers to stop. I reached over and dragged the plastic ice chest into my room. It was heavier than I'd expected. If it did contain drugs, there must've been a ton of them. I patted at my hips out of instinct before I remembered that I didn't have pockets in these shorts. "I'm sorry, I don't have my wallet right here to give you anything—if you want to wait, I can look—"

He shook his head. "Nope, not a problem. Lady took care of me already. You just. . ." He pointed in the general direction of the bed. "You should probably lay down or something. Maybe you need what's in the cooler, huh? Check it out." He looked all around again, and I felt his uneasiness steal over me like a slickness. "I'll catch you later."

He was gone before my door clicked closed. I dropped to my knees next to the ice chest and struggled to press the button to open it. My hands were shaking, although now that Shorty was out of sight, the numbers had quit shouting at me, and I couldn't see them anymore either.

The latch finally gave way, and the top swung down. I leaned to look inside.

Bags of red liquid were stacked neatly in two piles of three. Steam rose from them as the warmer air hit the dry ice. I leaned back, recoiling at the sight. *Blood? What the fuck?*

Did I need a transfusion? Gingerly I reached down to pick up one of the packets, wondering if I'd find tubing and needles beneath. Nothing. But honestly, did I really think I could give myself blood even if I had all equipment? Hell, I fainted at the sight of a paper cut. I was a total wuss when it came to medical shit.

I held the bag of blood in my hand, and a roaring need consumed me. It was a thirst unlike any I'd ever known, worse than when I'd run the Ironman Tri on the hottest day in June a few years back.

Follow your instincts, my friend.

I didn't seem to have any choice. All I could think of was the liquid in my grasp. I had to have it—now. There was a small circle near the top that was meant for a needle, I assumed. The plastic was thinner there, and I worked at it, tearing a little hole.

Once it had broken, I could smell the blood, and the pounding in my head was inescapable. I held the bag to my lips and sucked, hard, reveling in the cold metallic taste rolling over my tongue and down my throat.

I drained one bag and reached for another. When the second was dry, I dropped back, leaning against the end of the bed. The nausea was gone, and I felt stronger. More myself, and yet so different. I looked down at my hands, stained red with the few

drops I'd let escape my mouth, and horror hit me.
What had I done? What had I become?

Chapter 1

I'D BEEN WAITING a long time to eat at this elegant up-town restaurant, and now here I was, with succulent ten-derloin of beef and the most gorgeous man I'd ever seen. He was just about to reach across the table—to take my hand, I hoped, although it might have been to snag the last piece of beef from my plate—when instead he kissed me. I was confused; how had he reached my lips across the table, and why were his lips so wet and slobbery?

I blinked into sunlight only partly blocked by a small ball of white fur. His solemn brown eyes regarded me with hope, and his tail thumped against the bed. He kissed me again, and I giggled. The man and the meal might have both been a dream, but morning puppy love was my reality.

"Morning, Makani." I touched the soft fluff on his head. "Thanks for the wake-up kisses. Need to go out?"

The pup's tail wagged faster in answer. I swung my legs out of bed, groaning again, and paused momentarily to consider what I was wearing. An oversized tee completely hid my sleep shorts, but if I stuck to my tiny backyard, no one would see me. I decided it was a risk I could take.

Makani was only ten weeks old, and I didn't usually bother to put on his harness and leash for our first walk of the day, when the urgency was greatest. I scooped him up and hurried outside through the back door. Once we were on the small patch of grass that I generously referred to as my backyard, I deposited the pup on the ground.

"Okay, Makani." I used my best firm voice. "Be a good boy now. Come on, be a good boy."

According to the dog-training book, "be a good boy" was code for "go to the bathroom here and now." So far it had worked sporadically.

Makani was just getting down to business when I heard noise coming from the house next door. Instantly the dog's ears perked up, and before I could react, he took off in the direction of the sounds.

"Makani!" I yelled, giving chase. "Makani, you get back here! Heel! Stop!"

I came to a sudden halt just before I ran headlong into a huge sweaty man wearing a bright orange T-shirt emblazoned with the words "Don't Fuck with Number One". The front of his ball cap read "Marvelous Movers" in block print. He leaned on a dolly and looked down at me

"Hey there." A meaty hand on my shoulder steadied me. "That your dog?" He gestured with his head toward the deck on the back of my next-door neighbor's house, where Makani stood, alternately barking and whimpering.

"Yes." I hissed the word through clenched teeth, suddenly all too aware that I appeared to be dressed in only a T-shirt. My legs felt too long and exposed. I crossed my arms over my chest and tried to look casual. Relaxed.

"Hell, that ain't a dog!" Another burly mover rounded the truck to join my morning audience. "That's just an overgrown rat!"

Indignation overcame humiliation. "He is not a rat. He is a Maltese—and he's just a puppy." Summoning the tatters of my remaining dignity, I marched up the steps and grabbed Makani. My face burned as I ignored the jeering laughter of the two movers and turned to leave the deck.

"What's going on out there?" From within the darkness of the house, beyond the sliding glass door, I heard a husky voice. I squinted to make out a shape, but the man within didn't move close enough to the doors to be more than a shadow.

"Hey, Mr. Reilly—nothing, just one of your new neighbors comin' over to say hello." Mover Number Two's suggestive tone was barely veiled.

"No—my dog ran away over here—I'm sorry to bother you. I didn't realize anyone was living in the house. Not that my dog comes over here. Ever. Today was the first time—he heard people and just took off—" I realized I was babbling and shut my mouth with a snap. "Sorry."

Mr. Reilly—for that was apparently the name of my new neighbor—moved just a bit closer to the open door. I could see now that he was tall and had light hair, but his face remained shadowed.

"No problem." He spoke after a long silence. He turned to face the movers again, and through the shadows, I could see that while he wasn't what my grandma would call skinny, he wasn't a muscle-bound guy, either.

"If you don't need anything else from me at the moment, I'll be in the master bedroom, lying down. Just knock on the door when you're finished." He sounded tired, I thought. I wondered if he'd traveled a long way to get here. But before I could say anything or introduce myself properly, he disappeared into the darkness beyond the door.

The two moving men looked at each and shrugged. "Okay, whatever, boss," the first one called. "We'll take care of this." Both of them trudged toward the front of the house where I could make out the front of a large moving truck. Makani and I were forgotten on the deck.

I looked down at the puppy in my arms. He'd stopped struggling to get down and was snuggled against me.

"Created enough trouble for one morning, huh?" I nuzzled the top of his head. "Great way to greet our new neighbor. Did it escape your notice that he was much closer to my age than anyone else around here? Hmmm?" I climbed down the few steps and headed back toward my own back door, where I caught sight of my reflection in the glass. I groaned. I'd just met this new guy looking like I wasn't wearing any pants with my hair sticking out all over my head and pink night cream still in evidence below my eyes.

"Well, we made quite an impression, didn't we?" I muttered to Makani as I hauled him inside and closed the door behind us. "The first man under seventy to move into the neighborhood, and I meet him looking like a skank. A skank with pink eye."

The pup squirmed, and I let him down, watching absently as he scampered over the tile into the kitchen. He glanced over his shoulder to see if I were following him to dish up the morning dose of wet food.

"I shouldn't give you anything." I tried to put on my stern face even as I walked toward the fridge. "After that stunt you pulled. . .it should be bread and water for you."

The dog sat on his haunches and grinned up at me, his tongue lolling to one side.

"Oh, whatever." I dug around for the canned food and spooned it into his plastic bowl. "Just don't do that again. You can't go running off to the neighbors' houses. I'll get a bad rep as a puppy mama."

Makani barely spared me a glance as he gobbled up the food. Clearly good neighbor relations weren't at the top of his priority list.

I waited until he'd finished eating and then put him into the crate so that I could shower in peace and dress in my daily uniform of shorts, a loose T-shirt and flip flops. Working at home in Florida definitely had its advantages; no suits, no high heel shoes and no frustrating commute. Just me, my laptop and my camera, and whatever ingredients had to go into the dish of the day.

Just as I was about to fire up the computer, my doorbell rang. I stood up fast, wondering if it could possibly be my new neighbor, stopping in for a cup of sugar. Or to declare his undying love for me. Or even just his unbridled lust. Whichever, I was cool with it.

Sadly, a peek out the window told me that my visitor was not of the hunky new neighbor variety. The person standing on my stoop was decidedly female and a good forty years my senior.

I opened the door, smiling. "Hey, Mrs. Mac. What's up?"

She grinned up at me from below her fluffy gray bangs. "I just thought I'd stop by and make sure you had that terrifying monster dog of yours under control, you hussy, you!"

I swallowed a sigh. "So I take it that the story of my morning dash is already making the rounds, huh?"

"Sweetie, it was the hot topic at canasta this morning. Supposedly we have a new neighbor who's right around your age, and you're already throwing yourself at him. Dolores Sayers said she looked out her window and saw our very own Jackie O'Brien outside half-naked, flirting with the moving men. Becky Donavon said no, you forced your dog over there and tried to sweet-talk your way into the new fellow's house, wearing nothing but a tight shirt and a smile."

"Oh, for the love of Mike." I stood back, opening the door wider. "Come on in, and I'll set the record straight."

She followed me back into the kitchen, huffing a little as her white sneakers squeaked on the tile. "Are you cooking today?"

"Yeah. I was just about to look at the recipe." I pulled out a chair for her and pointed to the glossy hardcover book on the table. "Check out this one."

"Oh, boy. What's the title?" She reached for it and scanned

the cover. "*Feeling French and Frisky On The Cheap.*" She rolled her eyes. "Good Lord, what next? What ever happened to the basics? When your grandmother and I were young marrieds, the cookbooks had practical names. Like *Cooking on a Budget*. Or *Quick and Easy Meals for the New Wife.*" She tapped the glossy cover on the table. "This sounds like it can't decide whether it's a recipe book or a sex manual."

"Mrs. Mac!" I shook my head. "Honestly."

She poked my arm. "When I was your age, being American and frisky was enough for us. And what does cheap have to do with it? Doesn't cost anything to be frisky."

"It's these editors. They're always looking for a more outrageous name than the last so they can sell more books." I poured us each a cup of coffee and set down the mug in front my neighbor. "The chick who wrote this one has a show on the local cable station in Orlando. I guess she knows someone who knows someone at the magazine, and the next thing you know, I'm reviewing it."

"Hmph. What're you going to make?"

"Cute and Cocky Coq Au Vin."

Mrs. Mac raised her eyebrows. "You're putting me on. It's not really called that."

I laid my hand on my heart. "Swear to God. Can you believe it?" I sipped my coffee. "I don't know how I'm ever going to be taken seriously as a food writer when I have to make stuff like this."

"Maybe you don't have to worry about that any more. Maybe you'll hook yourself the man next door and be set for life."

I snorted. "First of all, what makes you think I need a man to be set for life? Second, maybe he's a total deadbeat, and he'd want me to support him, not the other way around. And last, with my luck he's either taken or gay. Or he could be a lot older than he looked. I didn't get a very clear view."

"Nah, he's not. I got the whole skinny on him from Poor Myrtle." Poor Myrtle was thus called because many decades before, when she was only eighteen, she'd gotten married in haste and subsequently repented at leisure, as the saying went. Her erstwhile groom ran off after a month of marriage, and Myrtle never got over it. She didn't ever remarry or even date, according to the Golden Rays scuttlebutt. Of course, what they didn't mention was that after her marriage debacle, she'd studied real estate and established her own agency in Pennsylvania. When retirement age rolled around, Poor Myrtle sold her business in a multi-million dollar deal and moved to Florida. She was bored down here, though, so she kept a desk in an agency and dabbled in the local housing market. Poor Myrtle, indeed.

"Oh, really? What does Poor Myrtle have to say? And why am I only hearing about this now? You could've told me before. I had no idea anyone was even moving in today."

"I didn't know, either. Apparently, his name is Lucas Reilly. He's Ellen's nephew. Poor Myrtle said Ellen left the house to him, and he told Myrtle he was moving down, but she figured he'd change his mind and just sell it. That's why she didn't say anything before now. She didn't want to get our hopes up, since she never thought anyone as young as him would want to live down here with all us old fogeys."

I tilted my head. "Hello? What does that say about me?"

She reached across and patted my hand. "Oh, honey, that's different. You're one of us."

"Thanks." Belonging was nice, sure, but being considered part of the crowd when the average age of that crowd was pushing ninety wasn't what I was going for.

"Anyway, he decided to come down and live here." She leaned forward, as thought someone might hear us in my kitchen with all the windows closed. "He's a college professor. Or he was, but now he moved down here so he can write a book. Isn't that a coincidence? He's a writer, like you want to be."

"Mrs. Mac, you know I *am* a writer already, right?"

"Of course I do. I just mean, he writes books. Or he will." Mrs. Mac was of the opinion that the only writing that counted was inside two hard covers. My job as a cookbook reviewer for *Food International* didn't qualify me for the title.

"Did Myrtle say anything. . .else about him?" I was trying to be subtle, which didn't always work with my friend.

She cast her eyes upward, thinking. "He's from New Jersey, he's not married, and she's pretty sure he's straight. Hard to tell about that over the phone, though."

"True enough." But she'd at least delivered the single part. Or at least not married. Not that I was necessarily willing to take anyone's word for that.

"So what do you think?" Mrs. Mac pushed her coffee cup to the side and leaned forward across the table.

"What do I think of what?" I knew damn well what she meant, but no way was I having it spread around that I was chasing after the new neighbor. Apparently enough rumors were already flying.

"This is your chance! How many times does the perfect guy move in right next to you? Not often, I'm here to say. Not often at all. Go for it." She winked at me. "Unless you already have a plan in mind? Was that what this morning was all about?"

I flushed. "No. This morning was about Makani deciding to go on a mad run when he was supposed to be taking care of business in his own yard."

"Were you really half-naked?"

"Of course not. I was wearing shorts and my Giants T-shirt." I finished my coffee. "Not my first choice of attire for meeting new people, but definitely not half-naked. Not even a quarter naked."

"That's a shame." Mrs. Mac wagged her head. "Might've worked in your favor. No one else in this block would have the guts to show up almost nude on the new guy's deck."

Even the thought of that scenario—my decidedly senior neighbors parading naked on anyone's deck—made me mildly nauseated, so I pushed it to the back of my mind and stood up. "Besides, I'm not man-hunting. I'm sure he's great, but I don't need to stalk the guy the next door. I've got plenty of chances to meet people."

"Sure, but men under 80 who're unattached and practically fall right into your lap?" She raised her eyebrows. "And I know you're not man-hunting, but Jackie, it's been five years since Will. Four since Maureen passed. You've been languishing down here, and it's time to move on. You don't want to end up like Poor Myrtle, do you?"

"God, no! What a horrible thing to say to me. Don't you know that's what haunts my nightmares?" I shuddered. "But I'm still not desperate. I don't need to jump the bones of the first available male who crosses my path."

"Okay, whatever you say, sweet cheeks." She pushed herself to stand up, too. "But if you were to decide to make a good impression, remember what my mama always said: the fastest way to a man's heart is through his stomach. And since you just happen to be cooking today. . .well, I guess you'll figure it out. Right?"

"I'm sure. Thanks for stopping by."

She waved her hand as she headed for the front door. "No, thank you for the coffee. And the scoop. I'll make sure everyone understands you weren't prancing around in your birthday suit. We have bingo tonight, so it should be easy to spread the word there."

"Awesome." The door slammed shut behind her, and I slumped back in my chair. Despite what I'd said to Mrs. Mac, I had to admit that the temptation of a single guy right next door who happened to be closer to my age than anyone else in a ten-block radius was pretty strong. And she did have a point: the kitchen was my happy place, and cooking was my secret weapon. Why not welcome my possibly-hot-new-neighbor by delivering a gourmet meal right to his door. . .and since I had to make this coq-au-vin recipe today anyway, there was apparently no time like the present.

"Watch out, Mr. Used-To-Be-College-Professor-Who-

Now-Wants-To-Be-A-Writer." I glanced out my kitchen window toward the house next door, where my two moving men buddies were still toting boxes. "Some Cute and Cocky Coq Au Vin is coming your way."

Chapter 2

MY KITCHEN SMELLED like heaven. Between the garlic and onions, the thyme and the wine. . .Mr. Lucas Reilly wouldn't know what hit him when he tasted this dish. The names might've been corny, but the cookbook author had done a good job with the recipes themselves. She was getting a five-star review in my column.

With the aroma still surrounding me, I sat down in front of my laptop at the kitchen table and pounded out the article. Writing these things didn't take long anymore; I'd perfected the balance of snark and self-deprecating humor, and my readers got a kick out of my food adventures. Nothing was off-limits, including my unplanned dash across the yard this morning.

. . .so imagine my surprise when the house next door wasn't vacant as I'd thought. In fact, two big ol' men were moving furniture into it from a truck parked at the curb. Yeah, those dudes got an eyeful of yours truly, prancing after the pup in just my PJs. My very scanty PJs. It's enough to scar a girl.

So in my need to wipe this mortifying memory from my brain,

I decided to indulge in a little culinary therapy. Today it took the form of an intriguing offering from Raya Johnson's cheeky new cookbook Feeling French and Frisky On The Cheap. Since I was clearly feeling quite frisky, I tried out the Cute and Cocky Coq Au Vin. Oh. . .my. . .Julia Child. I wish I could send you each just a little bite. Of the chicken, you naughty girls and boys. Get your minds out of the gutter.

I shared the recipe, added the author's bio and picture and then sprinkled in my own photos of the prep process. When my timer went off, I arranged one serving on the stark white plates I kept for food staging, added a little garnish and snapped a few last photos before I sent the whole kit and caboodle off to my editor.

Like many magazines, *Food International* had gone digital. A glossy edition went out once a quarter, while my column appeared on our website every week. I could do it in my sleep at this point. The writing wasn't going to win me any Pulitzer prizes, but it was a living. Or at least part of a living: it paid me enough that I could make ends meet, thanks to my grandmother's generosity in bequeathing me both this house and enough money to cover the annual taxes.

And clearly I'd been overlooking the perk of having gourmet food that I could share with potential hot guys. I arranged the chicken and vegetables in a white casserole dish and fastened the matching lid on top. I'd made one of my favorite loaves of crusty Italian bread, and I wrapped that in a wide linen napkin. Finally, I pulled a bag of washed greens from the fridge, tossed them in a small glass bowl with some chunky tomatoes, artichoke hearts and avocado and covered it with plastic wrap. My own homemade vinaigrette was in a small bottle, tucked next to the salad. Everything went into a sturdy wicker basket, along with a small bag of crunchy croutons.

Now that it was time to carry the meal over, nerves fluttered in my stomach. What if he thought I was crazy? And not in a fun, I-like-that-girl way? But more like obsessive-stalker-neighbor crazy? I caught sight of my reflection in the hallway mirror. My dark hair was up in a pony tail, my default style for cooking. My green eyes were serious and just a tad worried. I'd changed out of the cooking-splattered shirt I'd worn all day and into a clean black shirt with my denim shorts. I looked decent; not drop-dead, jaw-hanging gorgeous, but not completely repulsive either. Not bad for thirty-something, either.

I bit my lip, thinking, shifting the basket from one hand to the other. The house was silent; the entire neighborhood was quiet. It was late afternoon, and all of my senior friends were out catching early bird specials. In one of those rare moments of absolute clarity, I had a sudden image of my life, and what it might be if nothing changed. I'd live here in this house for the rest of my days, watching the people around me die one by one, until all the houses had turned over to new elderly folk. Eventually I'd stop being the young one in the neighborhood. I'd be part of the crowd. Just like Mrs. Mac had said today.

I'd grown lazy in the past few years. I couldn't remember the last time I'd gone out with anyone close to my own age; my best friend still lived in New York, and it'd been months since we'd seen each other. I wasn't above a game of canasta or bingo with the ladies on the block, but even those outings didn't appeal to me lately. Since Will. . .I pushed away the thought of that particular betrayal. It wasn't new, and it wasn't exactly pain, but what had gone down with my once-upon-a-time fiancé had definitely made me gun shy. Or maybe more accurately, guy shy.

So what did I have to lose by bringing a fabulous home-cooked meal to my new neighbor? Absolutely nothing. I gripped the basket a little tighter and strode out before I had a chance to change my mind again.

I couldn't tell whether or not he was home. I'd seen a dark sedan in the driveway earlier, and I assumed it belonged to him. The driveway was empty now, but it could have been in the garage attached to the house. I walked up the pavers that led to his front door and rang the bell without giving myself a second chance to over think this.

For a few moments, the house remained quiet. There wasn't any sound of stirring, no muffled noise of a television or footsteps. I was just about to leave the basket on the porch when the door swung open. I jumped back, my heart pounding in surprise.

"Can I help you?" The voice was a little less strained, a little deeper than I remembered it being this morning. But stop the presses, because the voice was the least of my focus. In the brighter light of late afternoon, the guy who'd seemed vaguely attractive while standing in the shadows was actually smoking hot. Dark blond hair looked like it was on the verge of needing to be cut, with a few wavy bits falling just above wide brown eyes. There was something about those eyes, some emotion I couldn't read. Caution that was nearly wariness overshadowed his expression, as his mouth tightened and his jaw clenched. He glanced over my shoulder, as though he were looking for something else. Or someone else.

"Uh, yeah. I mean, no, I can help you. Eat. Food. I brought you food. Dammit!" I swallowed and started over. "Hi, I'm your next door neighbor. I wanted to say welcome to the block. And I brought you dinner." I hefted the basket and thrust it forward.

His nose twitched. "It smells. . .delicious. Thanks, uh. . ." His voice trailed off, and he raised one eyebrow.

"Jackie." I juggled the basket, and he grabbed it from me, setting it down just inside the doorway. "Jackie O'Brien."

"Hello, Jackie." His lips quirked up on one side, and a dimple popped out on his left cheek. "Nice to meet you. I'm Lucas Reilly."

"I know." God almighty, what the hell was wrong with me? I sounded like a smarmy seven-year-old. "I heard the movers this morning call you Mr. Reilly. And news travels fast around here. Your realtor has loose lips."

Lucas rolled those captivating eyes. "Yeah, she gave me the third degree. I figured all the info would make the rounds." He glanced over my shoulder, an anxious frown on his face and then forced his attention back to me. He leaned one forearm against the door jam, and beneath the tight green T-shirt, I could see the flex of muscles. Nice. "Uh, so. . .what's for dinner?"

"Cock au vin." My mouth had apparently decided to act independently of my brain today. "I *mean*, coq au vin. Sorry. It's the name of the recipe. Silly, I know, but some of these cookbooks are just ridiculous."

"So, chicken, huh?" Lucas sniffed again. "And lots of garlic."

I shrugged. "A little, not a lot, I'd say. Why? Don't you like garlic?"

He hesitated. "I used to. But lately it makes me sick."

Fabulous. "Sorry. I guess I should've checked with you before I cooked. I've never heard of a garlic allergy."

He held up a hand. "No, really. How could you've known? It's fine if I don't eat the cloves themselves. I think, anyway. Like I said, it's kind of a new, uh, symptom. I appreciate it, really."

"Okay." There was pause, a silence chock full of awkward, which was my cue for more blurting out words. "I'm a writer, too."

"Oh, really?" He smiled, focusing on me, and ooh-la-la, there was that dimple again. "I guess the realtor let that slip, too. About me writing a book, I mean."

"Yeah, she did. That's really cool."

"So what do you write? Jackie O'Brien. . .I don't know your name off the top of my head. Or do you use a pseudonym?"

"No, I don't. And I haven't actually published a book. Not yet. I'm a columnist for *Food International.*"

"Oh." Understanding dawned on his face. "So the cooking. . ." He pointed down to the basket. "The writing and the cooking go together for you?"

"Yeah, it's kind of my thing. I review cookbooks by making a few of the recipes in them, and then I talk about how easy or difficult it is for the average cook to translate the meals in their own kitchens." I grinned. "Full disclosure: your meal tonight is going to show up on the magazine's web page next week. You know, two birds, one stone."

"One chicken, in this case." Lucas smiled, too, and I had to get a grip on myself to keep from melting into a puddle right there on his front porch. I struggled for something witty to say.

"Sorry about my dog this morning. He's never taken off like that. At least, not first thing in the morning. I usually keep him on a leash if we're outside, but I'm not used to anyone being over here. No one has lived here for a while."

He nodded. "No big deal. I like dogs. Just glad he didn't get run over by the moving men."

"Nah, only crushed by their derision." I smirked when Lucas tilted his head. "You know, they said he wasn't much of a dog."

"Oh, did they? Well, those two weren't exactly the Westminster Kennel Club. Hell, they weren't even the greatest movers." He sighed, running a hand through his hair. "You should see how much broken crap I have now, thanks to them."

"Moving sucks." Standing on the stoop was getting awkward, and I shifted to lean against the railing that ran along the edge of the porch. Lucas started to say something, but before I could hear him, the wrought iron creaked and gave way. My balance gave way with it, and for one moment that would be burned into my mind forever, I struggled to keep from falling, arms wind-milling in what must have been a cartoon-like fashion. I lost the battle and tumbled ass-first into one of the overgrown bushes that surrounded the porch.

I lay there for several seconds, hoping that maybe the stupid bush would just swallow me up the rest of the way. It was the only graceful exit open. But when I opened my eyes, I could see Lucas gaping down at me through the green leaves and twisted branches.

"Oh, my God. Are you all right?" He took one step forward and then stopped, his brow wrinkling and his mouth set again, as though he smelled something less-than-pleasant. Or as if he were in pain, which seemed strange, given the fact that I was the one lying in the shrubbery.

"I think so." I moved my hand until it hit ground and tried to push myself up. "Luckily this bush broke my fall. Ouch!" I winced and lifted my arm, where a thorn had taken up residence.

"Here." Lucas extended his hand down to me, finally. I took it, not failing to notice the strength in his grip as he hauled me up. His frown deepened as he stared at me, confusion clouding his eyes. He held my fingers between his for a little longer than was necessary, and my heartbeat picked up. It had been a long time since a man had held my hand, and if it took a clumsy dive into the greens to make it happen, I was okay with that now.

Before I could do anything completely irredeemable, like stand on tiptoe to kiss him, Lucas dropped my hand and stepped back. His face had shuttered closed, but I saw his Adam's apple bob as he swallowed.

"Uh, nothing's broken, right? I'm sorry about that. Myrtle the realtor said something about the rail needing to be replaced, but I completely forgot about it. You're the first person to come to the front door."

"Always happy to identify potential hazards." I rubbed my hip, thinking I was going to have a colorful bruise there by the morning. "I'm sorry I crushed your bush."

He waved his hand. "Nah, I'll probably get rid of them anyway. I'm planning to do some work around here, bring it up-to-date a little. I guess I found my first project."

"Great. Well. . ." I glanced behind him at the door. "I should let you eat your dinner while it's hot. It still should be. Hot, I mean." I brushed a few lingering bits of green out of my hair. "And I think I'll limp home and soak my injured pride."

Lucas smiled again, though it didn't quite reach his eyes. "Hey, don't worry about it. You made quite a first impression."

I shook my head. "That's me. First I run into your backyard in my pajamas, chasing a dog, and then I nosedive into your

25

plants. Bet you can't wait to see my third act."

His lips curved up into an almost-leer. "Is that what you were wearing? One of the movers said you had on nothing but a T-shirt and smile."

I closed my eyes, feeling red creep up my neck. "I had on shorts underneath it. But that's just great. I'm glad I could give your movers a thrill, too."

"Hey." He reached out to lay his hand on my shoulder, but I caught the briefest hesitation in his movement, almost as though he were afraid to touch me. "Really, don't sweat it." He dropped his arm and moved back inside the house. "Thanks again for the food. I'll bring your dishes back, okay?"

"Sure. Enjoy it." I waited to see if he would step up and invite me inside after all, but he only forced another smile and sketched a wave in my direction before he closed the door.

I turned and made my way across the yard toward my own back door. I didn't dare look around to see if any of my neighbors were peeking out their windows; my only hope was that no one else had witnessed that little adventure. Of course, it would give them something to talk about tomorrow at book club.

"Yep. I'm not kidding. Ass-over-teakettle into the bushes." I tucked my feet under me on the sofa and held the phone away from my ear as my friend Leesa howled with laughter.

"Oh, sweetie. . .I'm sorry. I know you must've been mortified. But really. . .the mental image is priceless. None of your elder friends got a video of it on her phone?"

I snorted. "Very few of them have mastered the science of using their phones for making calls, let alone for shooting video. No, I think I'm probably safe from showing up on YouTube, thank heavens for small blessings."

"That's a shame. It might make you an internet star."

"I think I'll pass, thanks." I glanced out the window. The house next door was dark, save for a single light on the porch. I wondered if Lucas had gone to bed early, or if he'd gone out. He didn't seem like the clubbing type from our brief interaction, but appearances could be deceiving. And maybe he did have a girlfriend down here, after all. Poor Myrtle the realtor wasn't known for being infallible.

"Jacks, are you there? Hellooooo?" Leesa yodeled into the phone.

"Yeah, sorry. What were you saying?" I shifted so that my back was to the window. I wasn't going to turn into the nosy next-door neighbor.

"I was asking about the guy. The one you took dinner to before you did the tumble act."

"Oh, umm. . ." I closed my eyes. "He's a college professor from New Jersey. Looks about our age, tall, dark blond hair, brown eyes. Oh, and get this, Leese—he's got a dimple. On his left cheek."

"Oooh, baby. So basically he's a hottie. What about his personality? Did he seem cool?"

I frowned. "Yes. Well, mostly. He was fine most of the time, but then he'd go kind of bizarre. Like he was waiting for someone. Tense about something."

"Hmm." Leesa put on her suspicious voice. "A girlfriend? A wife?"

"No, I don't think so. It was more like he was afraid of something."

"Oh, God, Jacks, maybe he's in witness protection. He used to be a mobster, and now he's an informant. You're living next door to someone who sang like a canary."

I rolled my eyes. Leesa could tend toward the dramatic now and then. "Right. So he moved to his aunt's house. Because that's the last place the hit men would look."

"Don't be silly. It's not really his aunt's house. That's just his cover."

"Maybe. Or. . ." I played with a loose thread on the seam of the couch. "He said something to the movers this morning about having to lie down. He stayed inside when Makani ran over there and just talked to them through the door. Oh, and tonight he said he couldn't eat garlic, that it's a new symptom. Could he be sick? Like one of those mystery illnesses, where he's got to stay away from people?"

"Or maybe he got bitten by a radioactive spider, and he's afraid to show you his web shooter. Do you want to see his web shooter, Jacks? Did his dimple make you hot for Spidey?"

"Shut up, bitch. What are you, twelve? I'm trying to be serious here."

"No, you're obsessing over someone you just met. Talk about middle school. You're analyzing everything he said and did, just like you did with Joey Crocker in seventh grade, when you were sure you were going to marry him and have tiny Crocker babies."

I sighed. "Joey Crocker just sold his internet start-up business for a cool six million. I should've held out for him, even after he called me Jack O'Lantern."

"How on earth do you know that?"

"Because it's on the class Facebook page. You know, the one you're too good to mess with, so you just get all your news from me. Someone posted a link to an article in the *Journal*."

"Huh." Leesa's interest was minimal and short-lived.

I heard the shuffle of papers through the phone. "Are you at work?"

"Maybe."

"You are. At eight-thirty at night."

"You don't make partner by going home at five."

"You need to get a life."

"I'm not the only one, toots. When's the last time you went any place but the grocery store?"

I huffed out a breath. "I went out to lunch at Leone's on Monday."

"By yourself?"

"No." I let it sit a beat, and then I gave in. "With Mrs. Mac."

"That doesn't count. Jacks, ever since you moved to Florida, you've stopped living. Before that even. Since Will. And now you've let working at home make you a hermit. You need to get out, go to clubs. Be a strong, confident woman. Meet people. People who don't remember the Great Depression."

"I'm not a hermit. And I'm sorry, I think finding out my fiancé was already married should qualify me to take a little recovery time when it comes to dating." I pressed my lips together. The memory didn't hurt so much, but I still didn't like it. "You should come down here, and we'll go out together. When was your last vacation?"

Leesa sighed. "I had a root canal over lunch five months ago. Does that count?"

"Nope. You have to actually go a whole day without being at the office."

"Then you should come up here and get some culture. We'll go to the museums and Bloomingdales and Broadway. C'mon, it's been way too long since you've been home."

"You sound like my mom and dad. Who, by the way, do come visit me every once in a while, unlike other people I know."

"Yeah, yeah, yeah. When I'm named partner, I'm taking three weeks off, and the first thing I'll do is swing down to the land of the early bird special. But for now, I've got to go."

"Fine. If it turns out my neighbor is a mob informant on the run, and someone rubs me out by mistake, you'll have to live with the guilt."

"I'll try to soldier on. 'Night, Jacks. Love you."

"Love you too, Leese."

I dropped my cell phone on the table next to the sofa and lay my head against the cushion. The house was silent except for the hum of the air conditioning. Makani was sprawled out on the tile floor, his little belly heaving up and down with his rapid puppy breaths.

It was too early for bed and too late to do anything else. I picked up the TV remote and flipped through the channels, surfing over endless reruns, news updates and infomercials before I clicked it off with a frustrated sigh.

I let my eyes slide from the blank television screen to the window. Lucas's house still appeared to be empty. If he'd already gone to sleep, it supported my tragic-illness theory. Poor Myrtle *had* said he'd left his career as a college professor to write a book. Maybe it was because he knew his time was limited. He'd come down here, leaving his friends and family behind so they wouldn't have to watch his steady, inevitable decline. He planned to be alone, to live out his last few months—weeks?— by himself.

But he hadn't counted on me. I'd be there for him, supplying chicken soup, pots of hot tea, a hand to hold when it all became too much. In my fantasy, whatever he had wasn't contagious, so hand-holding was okay. We'd both know that if only things were different, if only life were fair, we'd have met under better circumstances and lived happily ever after. It was tragic, but we'd be strong. I'd keep a brave face to the end, and when his eyes closed for the last time, I'd finally let myself weep and whisper the words neither of us had dared to utter. . .*I lo*—

The doorbell chimed, and I jumped so far I nearly tumbled again, this time off the sofa. I clapped my hand to my heart in true Italian girl fashion, just like my mom and my Nonna always did when they were startled. Genetics did work.

Doorbells after nine in my neighborhood were not a good thing. The last time I'd had a late-night visitor was when Mr. Grover down the street had a stroke and fell in his bath. He'd managed to trigger his life alert alarm, but when the paramedics arrived on the scene, the only the name they could find for his emergency contact was mine. I was the lucky person who got to sit with him in the back of the ambulance and hold his hand as we sped to the hospital. I found out later that most everyone on the block had listed me as the person to be called in case of emergency. Mrs. Mac thought that was completely reasonable.

"Well, dear, you're younger than us. I could have one of the other neighbors, but what if she dies and I forget to update it? And all my family lives so far away. I knew you wouldn't mind."

Still, I was a woman living alone, and I couldn't be too careful. If an attacker chose my house to invade, Mrs. Mac wasn't going to hear me scream, and apparently Lucas wasn't home to come to my rescue. Plus, there was the whole tragic-illness deal. Although the idea of him saving me at great risk to his fragile health was kind of romantic.

I stood next to my front door and pushed aside the sheer curtain that covered the narrow windows adjacent to it, peering through and hoping the person ringing the bell didn't see me.

Unless she had eyes in the back of her head, she didn't. The petite, dark-haired woman standing on my front porch had her back to me as she glanced around her. One hand was on the small of her back, rubbing as though it ached. The other leaned against the side of the house. She didn't seem like a threat, so I turned the deadbolt and opened the door.

"Oh, thank God. I was afraid you weren't here, and you're my last delivery of the day." She arched her back, facing me fully, revealing a very round pregnancy bump. "My feet are killing me. I know it's late, but this one just came in, and all my boys had left for the night. I could've called one of them back, but I saw the address, and you're right on my way home. So I decided to just make the drop myself."

She bent over, lifted a white and red cooler and handed it to me. "Here you go. Ms. Reilly? Mrs. Reilly?"

I took the box automatically while my brain tried to catch up. "I—um—"

"My name's Nichelle DeWare. I own the company that'll be delivering for you. I got your paperwork right here." She twisted a little and dug into the big black leather bag that hung from her shoulder. "It was all set up for you, but you'll need to confirm a few things and set up times and so on. It's easy enough, and if you'd rather do it online, the website is on the cover page. I highlighted it."

I finally found my voice. "I think there's a mistake. I'm not expecting a delivery, and I'm not Ms. Reilly." My heart sunk; so was there a Mrs. Reilly after all? Did Lucas have a wife?

"No, I'm sure that's right." Nichelle rubbed her belly as she squinted at the paper in her hand. "L. Reilly, it says right here. 3505 Mitchell Terrace. One cooler, twice a week. O negative."

My mind tripped over all information pouring in. "No, see, this is 3503." I pointed over her shoulder to the faded number on the front of my garage. "My name isn't Reilly. But my new neighbor, right over there next door, is Lucas Reilly. I bet that's who you want."

The woman struck her forehead with the heel of her hand. "Oh my God, I'm an idiot." She peered up at me through the dimness of my porch light. "Do you have kids?"

"Uh. . ." This question felt oddly random, but on the other hand, nothing had made sense since I'd opened the front door. "No, I don't."

Nichelle nodded. "See, what happens is, you get pregnancy brain, and you lose brain cells. No one tells you this when you're thinking of the cute little bundle, but it's the truth." She sighed, heavily, and shook her head. "I got two other kids at home. They're two and four, and I love them like mad, but I'm telling you, they suck it all away. I'm seven months along with this one, and it's only getting worse."

I had no idea how to respond to this. "I'm sorry?"

"No, I'm sorry for bothering you." She pointed at Lucas's house. "So that's where Mr. Reilly lives?"

"Yeah, but I'm not sure he's home. The house has been dark all night." I spoke without thinking again, and I wanted to bite off my tongue. *Not that I'd been watching or anything.*

But Nichelle didn't seem to notice. "Well, crud. He was expecting this delivery so you'd think. . ." She turned back to look at me again. "See, that's another thing. I used to be able swear with the best of them. I had a potty mouth that got me almost kicked out of high school 'cause I couldn't rein it in. But I had a kid, and suddenly shit, damn and hell become crud, dang and heck." She flashed me a wide smile. "But you don't have kids, and it's just us grown-ups here, so what the fuck, right? This guy needs to get his shit together, because I can't just leave the cooler on his step. That's not how this works. Damn men, you know? They just think the world revolves around them."

"Yeah, I guess. He knew you were coming?" I leaned out and peered around her.

"Well, not me, in particular, but he'd be waiting for a delivery." Her eyes narrowed as she followed my gaze. "Maybe he's just sitting in the dark? Or—oh, look. A light just went on." She bent over, letting out a soft groan as she gripped the cooler again. "So I'm sorry for disturbing your night, um. . ." She trailed off, question in her tone.

"Jackie. I'm Jackie O'Brien."

"Okay, nice to meet you, Jackie O'Brien." She cocked her head and stared at me. "You wouldn't by any chance be the same Jackie O'Brien who writes for *Food International*, would you?"

I'd never met anyone outside the magazine and my family or friends who recognized my name. "Yeah, I am."

Nichelle's mouth dropped. "Oh my GOD. I read your column every week. I never buy a cookbook you haven't reviewed. Okay, well, mostly I just like to read about you cooking, because you're funny as hell, you know? Wow. You're Jackie O'Brien."

I couldn't hide my grin. "Thanks so much. You have no idea how much this means." Inspiration struck me. "Hey, do you want a cookbook? Do you like to cook?"

"Yeah, I love it. That's why I follow you. Hell, yeah, I want a cookbook. Will you sign it?"

I had already turned around to pick up the book. "Sure,

33

but you know I didn't write the book, right?" I held up *Feeling French and Frisky on the Cheap*. "But I'll be reviewing a recipe from this book next week in my column."

"Oh my God, how cool is that. Yeah, I still want you to sign it." She watched me fumble for a pen. "It's Nichelle, like Michelle but with an N. Okay?"

I scrawled a brief inscription. "Here you go. And thanks for being a reader. Now and then I wonder if anyone's following."

She held up her right hand as though she were taking an oath. "Never miss a week, and I tell all my friends. And my mom reads you, too. Oh my God, they're going to die when they hear I met *the* Jackie O'Brien. Hand to God." She glanced over to Lucas's house. "I guess I better go make that delivery, but thanks so much for this." She lifted the book. "I can't wait to read what you made."

"It was nice to meet you."

"Oh, and hey. If you could. . .just forget about what I said, about the delivery and everything, okay? We're big on discretion. Our clients can be kind of funny about any of their business getting out. I have no idea what happens after I leave. None of mine, you know? But I can't afford for any of them to get jumpy and start canceling on me."

"Sure. Of course, I understand. Never happened." I made a zipper motion across my mouth.

"Awesome. Okay, catch you later. Thanks again."

I waved as she stalked back down my front walk and cut across the grass. For a pregnant lady, she moved pretty fast.

"Well, if that wasn't weirdest thing I've ever heard, it's got to be in the top five." Talking to myself was a bad habit, but at least most of the time I could pretend I was really talking to the dog. I looked down at him, still sacked out. "Glad you jumped up to protect me, oh fearless one."

He didn't even stir.

Chapter 3

AFTER I CLOSED the front door behind Nichelle, I turned off all the lights in my living room, sat down on the sofa in the dark and watched the house next door. Nichelle knocked on Lucas's door, and moments after he opened it, spilling light onto the porch, she disappeared inside.

I didn't move, but my mind was shouting. She'd said O negative. That had to be blood, right? So she was delivering blood? Who knew there was such a thing? And why in the hell did Lucas need blood? It supported my tragic-illness theory, though I wasn't sure I'd ever heard of even the sickest patients requiring blood that often. And wouldn't he have to have a medical professional give him a transfusion if he needed it?

About ten minutes after Nichelle went inside, the door opened again. She tossed a quick wave over her shoulder and stomped toward her car, which was still parked at the curb in front of my house. As she climbed in and started it up, Lucas leaned outside. He looked over toward my house, and I froze; it was impossible, but it felt as though he could see me across the yard and through my window.

A shiver ran down my spine. Maybe it wasn't really blood. If Leesa's witness protection theory were accurate, what if Nichelle was actually some kind of messenger, and I'd accidentally intercepted the package? Was O negative code? But that was crazy. Nichelle was seven months pregnant. She was the least likely candidate for a government agent. Or maybe that was the point.

Lucas stared for a few more moments before he stepped back inside and closed the door. The light on the porch went out, leaving our block in velvet darkness.

When I felt like it was safe to move, I checked the locks on the front and back doors, scooped up Makani and took him into my bedroom. And I'm not ashamed to say I locked that door, too, and kept one light burning all night.

The next morning, everything that had terrified me the night before seemed silly. There had to be a perfectly rational explanation for Nichelle and her delivery. She hadn't exactly come out and said she had blood in the cooler; I had inferred that, and I must've misunderstood. Or maybe there was a simple answer; the blood was needed for transfusions and they delivered it directly, but then a nurse would come and set it up. Or maybe she hadn't even said O negative.

I walked around muttering the two words to myself. "O negative. Ah nagative. Ah neg. Aneg ateeve." I couldn't come up with a single phrase that matched that one and actually meant something.

I kept a surreptitious eye on the house next door, but I didn't see Lucas or any visitors all morning. It was quiet.

At noon, I sat down and gave myself a stern talking-to. "Jackie, you're making a big deal about nothing. And you know why you're doing this? Because you have no life. *No life.* You're turning a new neighbor who, okay, might be a little odd, into a tragic hero or some kind of criminal. He's just a guy. Just guy who moved down here into his aunt's house. People probably thought it was weird when you moved into Nana's house, too. Well, maybe not so much since you took care of her here for a year before she died, but still. Now get your ass in gear and go somewhere. Get out, go see people, act like you're normal."

I decided I'd given myself good advice. I crated Makani, grabbed my keys and got in the car, not even sparing one glance next door. Or not much of one, at least. Since my stomach was growling, my first stop was Leone's, the old diner at the corner just outside our development.

Alfonso Leone and my Nana had been good friends since she'd moved to Florida. He was old-school Italian, with the charm and class that captivated all women from the age of two to ninety-eight. I'd fallen in love with him the minute Nana introduced us, and if he wasn't fifty years older than me, I knew we'd be making love in Venice even now. He'd been with me when my grandmother passed in the middle of the night before my parents could get there. He'd held my hand during the bleak days that followed, and he was one of the main reasons I'd chosen to stay in Florida.

The bell rang over the door, and the heads of six customers sitting at the counter swiveled toward me in unison. Al was standing just outside the swinging kitchen door, talking to one of the waitresses. He caught sight of me, and his smile bloomed.

"*Cara mia! Buon pomeriggio.* You here for lunch, sweetheart?"

I took a deep, appreciative sniff. "I could smell your pomodoro all the way from my front door, Al. I'm in the mood for some pasta."

He pointed to my regular booth, empty and waiting for me. "Sit down. I fix you right up." Al leaned into the kitchen and spouted off a string of Italian too fast for me to translate, but I caught the words *capellini* and *veloce*. He moved with agility that belied his eighty years as he filled a goblet with ice and water, adding a wedge of lime and a straw before he brought it to me. He slid into the seat across the table.

"So, what's wrong, *tesoro*? I can see it in your eyes. You're troubled. Is it the new man?"

I gaped at him. "What new man? What do you know?"

He flipped his hand, shaking his head. "Does not matter." When I tilted my head and stared, waiting, he sighed. "All right. You pull it out of me. Anna was in this morning with her card-playing group. They were talking about the new man who moved in next to you, and how maybe the two of you, eh, you know. . ." He waggled his eyebrows. "At last maybe you find the right one."

I slumped back on the padded bench. Mrs. Mac and her big mouth. "Really? You, too? I'm beginning to think you've all been looking at me like a lost cause, and I didn't even know it. The first eligible guy comes along, and you're ready to send me down the aisle."

"No, no. We just want you to be happy. *I* want you to be happy. To have what I did with my Elisabett, God rest her soul." He crossed himself, and instinctively I did the same. I'd never met his late wife, since she'd passed away long before even Nana had moved down here, but I'd seen pictures and heard stories enough to know that she'd been the love of his life.

I rested my chin on my hands. "Maybe not everyone is cut out to have that, Al. Maybe some people are meant to be on their own. Fend for themselves."

He humphed. "Maybe some people, but not you. You have so much joy to give, *cara*. I see you with people. You bring the sunshine, yes? You need someone to share that with. Someone so you won't always be so alone."

"I'm not lonely. I have you, and Mrs. Mac, and all the people in the community. And Leesa and my parents and Bret and Tim, too." My older brothers both lived within ten minutes of the house where we'd grown up. "I mean, yeah, I don't see them that much, but still, we talk. I'm not a hermit."

"No one is saying you are, sweetheart, but. . .ah! Here is your food. Thank you, Mary."

We both lapsed into silence as the waitress arranged a small green salad and a plate overflowing with angel hair and red sauce. Mary smiled at me and patted my shoulder as she left, making me wonder if she'd been in on the poor-Jackie conversation earlier, too.

"Eat now, we'll talk later." Al began to rise, and I reached across to lay a hand on his arm.

"No, don't go. I didn't mean to jump on you. It's just that you're not the first person in the last few days to say I need to get a life."

"We worry. Everyone loves you, and all your friends and family want to see you happy." *Before it's too late* was the part he left off, although it hung in the air between us.

"I appreciate that." I twirled a healthy bite of pasta around my fork. "But just because a man moves into the neighborhood doesn't mean he's the one for me." I closed my eyes and hummed a little as I lifted the fork to my mouth. "Oh, Al. This is like heaven."

"Of course it is. Someday, when you write my cookbook for me, that's what we'll call it. *Food Like Heaven*, yes?"

I nodded. "That's a perfect title. We need to jump on that. I can't keep reviewing other people's cookbooks when there's one just begging to be written, right?"

"Yes, and so much better than the others. I just read your column from last week. The book was called *Pasta for a Pittance*. Why do people write such nonsense? Food is the ultimate luxury. Even if you can't afford much, you can make a meal so good, it transports you."

"I wish you'd write that down. It could be our introduction to the cookbook." I took a sip of water. "We really need to get serious about this, Al. Just think of how huge it's going to be."

"Yes!" He smacked the edge of the table with his hand. "Let's make a plan. When does it work for you? Maybe we can start meeting in the afternoon, after the lunch rush but before dinner. Would that be okay?"

"That would be perfect." I pushed aside my plate and dug into the salad. "So what did Mrs. Mac tell you about Lucas?"

He smiled. "Nothing much. Just that he was younger, closer to your age. And that you ran over to meet him yesterday, dressed in your night clothes." Al's grin broadened, which told me he knew the truth and was choosing to tease me.

"Yup. Nothing on but a smile. Hey, if I'm going to catch a man, I need to pull out all the stops, right?" I bit into a tomato, and the juice spurted out, staining the white paper napkin on the table. It looked like a blood spatter pattern. Which reminded me . . .

"Al, do you know anything about the mob?"

His thick white eyebrows shot up to his hairline. "What?! Why would you ask me such a thing?"

"I just had some questions." I leaned in and lowered my voice. "I'm not saying you're connected with the mafia, but you know things. You knew a lot of people when you still lived up north."

"Everyone knows people. If you lived where I did, you knew someone who was connected. But you don't talk about it." He thumped at his chest. "*I* don't talk about it."

I rolled my eyes. "I'm not asking you to do an exposé, Al. I just wanted to pick your brain."

He sat back and closed his eyes, exhaling. "All right. Ask."

I glanced around us. The lunch crowd, already sparse since it was later, had dwindled to almost nothing. Still, I hunched my shoulders as I spoke. I didn't want to get anyone in trouble. "If someone was in witness protection, hiding out from the mob, how would the government contact them? Would they maybe use a messenger? Or do they just call people?"

Al wrinkled his forehead. "Why are you asking me about this? Are you in trouble?"

"No, not me." I folded my napkin, hiding the blood-red tomato stain. "Lucas. The new guy next door. He's. . .there's something odd, Al. I know I only met him yesterday, and maybe

40

I'm being dramatic and crazy, but it's just weird. He seems like he's afraid of something." I fiddled with the fork resting on the edge of my plate. "And then last night, this chick came over with a delivery. She came to my house by mistake, and when she realized it, she asked me to keep it on the down low."

Al spread his hands, shrugging. "Maybe it was something private. People are funny about their business, *cara*. Sometimes there are secrets, and it is better that they stay buried. Secrets that could only hurt other people." He looked down at the table, at his hands. "All of what you told me doesn't mean this man is a mob informant. There are a million other answers." His eyes narrowed. "Is he Italian?"

"No. At least his name isn't Italian. But isn't there an Irish mafia?"

Al laughed. "Perhaps, but that's beyond that my limited knowledge. This isn't like you, Jackie. What's the matter?"

I sighed. "I don't know, Al. Maybe you're right. I'm alone too much, and I have nothing but time on my hands." I dropped my head back to rest on the top of the bench. "Leesa says I should go back to New York for a while. I wonder if I should consider it."

"Not for good? We'd miss you too much if you moved away. But a little trip probably wouldn't hurt you. Go before it gets cold up there. You don't want to get stuck in the snow."

"I guess." The idea didn't appeal to me at all. I tried to convince myself that my reluctance had nothing to do with Lucas. "But we need to start your cookbook. I can't leave right now."

Al studied me. "You know what I think? I think you should go home, march over to the man's house and ask him out to dinner. Bring him here, and we'll fix you up right, huh? Tell him you want to get to know him better, welcome him to Florida. Who in his right mind could say no to you, *mia bella*?"

I stood and bent over the side of the booth to kiss his worn cheek. "And this is why I love you, Al. Why on earth weren't you born fifty years later?"

"Ah, did you ever think maybe you were born too late instead? But no, *cara*, I was meant to be with Elisabett. . .and there is someone out there for you, too." He winked and patted my hand. "Closer than you think, I bet."

"Sure, and with my luck, it'll turn out he really is in the mafia, and I'll have to decide between life on the run or living without my one true love."

"Don't talk like that." Al glanced around again. "Listen to me now, Jackie, you're half-joking, but even around here, there're people who take that very seriously. People you don't want to meet, and me, neither. So watch what you say." He stood up next to me and jabbed me in the ribs with his elbow. "Capiche?"

"Yes, sir." I hiked my purse onto my shoulder. "Add this to my tab, please?"

"You got it. And give me a call if you're going to come in tonight with the neighbor. I want to save you a good table."

"Will do. Let's plan to meet on Monday at three to start planning the cookbook, okay? I'll bring my laptop and some notes. You just bring your recipes."

Al beamed. "I cannot wait to tell the grandchildren that Poppy is going to be published. They'll never believe it."

"Well, pretty soon you'll be making the rounds of cooking shows, having signings at bookstores. . .I'll be cooking your food to review in my column. You're going to be huge, Al. And we'll all be able to say we knew you when." I blew him a kiss. "See you tonight. Maybe."

I talked myself into and out of asking Lucas to dinner on my drive home.

"You can do this. You're a strong, confident twenty-first

century woman. You're not a little girl. You've dated before. Just march right over there, smile big and say, 'Hey, Lucas. I'd like to take you to dinner tonight. I'll pick you up at six.'"

At the next stop light, though, the strong, confident woman fled the scene and left the freaked-out me behind.

"No way I can do this. I can barely string together two words when I'm talking to him. I don't make sense. I just fall off porches into bushes. Besides, if he wanted to eat dinner with me, he'd ask. The guy does the asking. And he just moved here. Like, just. He probably still doesn't have all his crap unpacked, and I'm asking him on a freaking date? Nope."

I turned into my driveway, and the choice about talking to Lucas was taken out of my hands. He stood at my front door, my basket in his hand as he pushed on the doorbell. My stomach rolled over. Lucas heard the car and turned, bracing his body, his face rigid. He was so clearly in a defensive stance that for a moment, I sat in the car and gaped.

When he realized it was me, he relaxed a little bit, arranging his face into careful neutrality and leaning against the side of my house. But I noticed he kept a white-knuckle grip on the handle of my basket.

I climbed out of the car, moving slowly, my eyes never leaving him. Something crackled in the air between us: an electricity and pull unlike any I'd ever known. Lucas didn't look away, but when I came within a few feet of the porch, he managed a smile.

"Hey. I was just returning your basket. And your dishes, of course. I didn't know if anyone was at home."

"Just Makani." I dug in my purse to find the house keys. "I ran over to Leone's to eat lunch. Come on in." I wasn't making that optional as I unlocked the door and swung it open. "Have you been to Leone's yet? It's the diner right outside Golden Rays. Best Italian food in Palm Dunes."

Lucas followed me inside. "No, I haven't been out much since I moved. You know, unpacking and setting everything up is time-consuming." I was aware of him checking out the living room as I hung my keys on the hook inside the door and set my handbag in the closet, but I didn't say anything else until I turned to face him again.

"How was the chicken?" I held out my hand for the basket. "Not too much garlic for you, I hope."

"Not at all. It was perfect." His fingers were warm beneath mine on the handle. "I enjoyed it. The only thing that would've made it better was company. I was really rude yesterday when you came by. I'm sorry I didn't invite you in to eat with me."

A kind of gladness swelled within me. "That's okay. It was just meant to help you on your first night in a new place, not so you had to entertain me." *Now would be the perfect opening to invite him to eat with me tonight.* I knew it, but I couldn't get out the words.

Lucas raked his hand over his hair. "I appreciate that. And I want you to know that under other circumstances, I'd love to have dinner with you. Get to know you more. I'm sure the fact that we're both sort of. . .anomalies in this neighborhood might give people certain ideas. And you seem to be a nice person. But right now, I've got stuff going on. I just—"

The bottom fell out of my stomach, and the room spun just slightly off-kilter. "Whoa, whoa. Please. Just hold it right there. What are you saying?"

Lucas stared at me, his brows drawn over his eyes. "I'm sorry, I'm not trying to be rude or hurtful. But I think it's best to be honest with you from the beginning."

"What made you think you had to be?" Damn it, tears of humiliation were forming in my eyes. This was ridiculous. I was too old to cry over a man I'd just met.

If Lucas had seemed uncomfortable before, now he looked downright pained. "I didn't want to say anything. . .but a few of your neighbors stopped in to see me today. They all mentioned how excited you were to have me here, living next to you, and that this could be your chance—look, I don't want to make you feel bad. I'm sure they meant well, and like I said, if things were different, I'd be really happy to take you out. Get to know you. But the way things are now, I just can't involve anyone else. It wouldn't be fair."

I closed my eyes. My surrogate family, the people who loved me and watched out for me. . .of course they'd taken matters into their own hands and visited Lucas today. They'd thought they were doing the right thing. I wasn't sure I'd ever been more touched and mortified at the same time.

"Look, Lucas, I think there's been some miscommunication. I brought you food last night because I had to make that recipe, and I thought it would be the neighborly thing to do. I'd have made dinner for you whether you were eighty or a woman. Plus, I felt bad about my dog running into your yard. But I promise you, I'm not hatching some scheme to trap you into—into dating me. Liking me, I guess. You're under no obligation here."

Lucas frowned. "But Mrs. MacConnelly and Mr. Rivers said. . ." He shook his head. "Okay, you know what? I'm just going to shut up right now. Obviously there's been some sort of misunderstanding." He took a step back away from me, toward the front door. "I'll say thank you for making me dinner, like I should've done from the beginning. And I'll leave it at that. Let's forget I ever said anything else. I'm sure I'll see you sometime." He wheeled around and headed toward the door.

I should've kept my mouth shut and let him go. But apparently strong, confident me had decided it was time to make herself heard.

"Why?"

Lucas stopped in mid-step, but he didn't turn around. He braced one hand on the corner of the wall. "Why what?"

"Why wouldn't it be fair to get to know me right now? Why aren't you free to have dinner with me, if you want?"

He began to answer, but I interrupted and kept talking.

"I mean, if I'm not your type, that's okay. But you haven't gotten to know me, so how can you be sure about that? All you can say for certain is that I cook—and actually, I'm a hell of a cook—and I'm a columnist, and I live right smack in the middle of a community of old people, and I'm a klutz who falls into bushes. I guess if you're used to dating twenty-something super-models, I might not appeal to you. But that's all you have to say. It doesn't have to be such a big deal."

Lucas laughed, a harsh bark devoid of humor. "Believe me, I don't date supermodels. I'm sure you're a terrific person, Jackie. What I've seen of you so far, I like. You're funny and interesting, and of course you're damned beautiful." He made a sound, deep in his chest that almost sounded like a growl. "It's complicated. It's nothing to do with you. It's my issues, and like I said. . .complicated."

Complicated. "Like crazy ex-girlfriend complicated? Or you have some rare disease? Or you're in witness protection? Or you're on a reality show, and you have to hide out until it airs and we find out you didn't get a rose?"

He turned around to face me again. "I'm not sure what the hell that means, but no. I can't give you any details. I don't think it's safe to get you involved, not when I myself don't even—" His face contorted, and his fingers gripped the wall. "I need to go. I'm sorry, Jackie. I have to leave now."

"But—" Whatever was going to come out of my mouth next was lost in the slamming of my front door. I stumbled to the window and watched Lucas sprint across the grass to his own porch, where he darted inside.

I sat down on the edge of my couch, my head spinning. What the hell was that? It was almost as though he'd gotten some internal signal, something that pained him. That would fit into the mystery-illness scenario, but he didn't look sick as he ran across our yards. And he said it wasn't safe to get me involved. But it couldn't be a matter of exposing me to a sickness since he wasn't afraid to be in the same house as me.

We hadn't even broached the topic of Nichelle and blood delivery. If anything, I had more questions than I'd had before our little talk.

I flopped back onto the sofa to take stock of what I'd learned. He'd said he'd ask me out if it weren't for this complication. He found me interesting and funny and—I grinned—beautiful. No, not just beautiful, but damned beautiful. His eyes had been open and honest as he'd said that, so I didn't think it was a line. There wouldn't be a reason for him to say that if it wasn't how he felt; he sure wasn't trying to get into my bed, or if he was, he had the most roundabout route of any guy I'd ever met.

Unless he had a beeper hidden on him somewhere that alerted him to mob danger, I thought Lucas's abrupt departure made the mafia scenario more unlikely. Which meant I was right back at square one. . .except now, I knew he found me attractive. *Damned beautiful.*

I held those words close to me all the rest of the day while I worked on preparing my coq au vin column to submit to my editor, perused the next cookbook in line for review and did my daily chores. All the while, I kept my eye on the house next door, watching for any movement, any visitors, or any more deliveries. There was nothing. The windows stayed dark as night fell, and when I finally gave up and went to bed at midnight, nothing stirred at all at Lucas's house. It was as though he had gone inside and vanished.

Chapter 4

"**MRS. MAC**, I cannot believe you did that. You went to his house and basically told Lucas he needed to ask me out? What came over you?"

We were standing in the narrow slice of grass that divided my house from hers. Mrs. Mac wore her gardening hat, as she'd been weeding her flowers when I came out to confront her.

"Oh, Jackie." She twisted off her gloves and glanced up me, guilt in her eyes. "I don't know what came over us. We met for breakfast at Leone's, and then we all went over to Sheila's to play gin. And one thing led to another, and I made us Bloody Marys. The next thing I knew, I was standing on the new man's porch, telling him what he'd be missing if he didn't ask you out. I'm sorry, honey."

I blew out a sigh. "*You* made the drinks, Mrs. Mac? Haven't we talked about that?" I loved this woman like she was my own grandma, but a bartender she was not. Her cocktail parties were legendary for the strength of the drinks. My dad privately called her Heavy-Handed Anna.

"I know, but no one else volunteered, and none of us was driving, so I thought it'd be okay." She looked positively contrite, and I knew I couldn't hold it against her.

"It's all right." I patted her shoulder. "I know you meant well. It just put Lucas in a bad position. And I'm afraid he thought I put you up to it."

"Oh, no." She shook her head. "No, I specifically remember that we all told him that you didn't know we were coming to see him. Earl even told him you'd probably be really mad if you knew it."

"Well, there's that." I swiped a hand across my forehead. "Don't worry. He made it crystal clear to me that he's not interested." That wasn't true, strictly speaking, but trying to explain something I didn't understand myself seemed like a losing battle.

"That's ridiculous. How could he not be interested in you?" Mrs. Mac put her hands to her hips and pursed her mouth.

"Step down, lady. I see that look in your eyes. Just let it go. I don't need any of you to fight my battles or find me a boyfriend. I might be younger than you, but I'm a big girl, all the same." I cocked my head at her. "Got it?"

She nodded. "Of course, Jackie. I won't do anything else." She held up her right hand in a loose approximation of the Girl Scout pledge position and nodded, her eyes wide.

"Okay." I kissed her smooth cheek. "You're off the hook. And I have a new cookbook to check out. Just arrived in the mail. I've got to see what epicurean delights I'll be sharing with my loyal readers next week."

The idea of loyal followers reminded me of Nichelle and her visit the other night. I'd awoken this morning determined to put Lucas, his mysterious complications and how *damned beautiful* he found me out of my mind. I didn't need drama, and I didn't need to throw myself at any man. At least, that is what strong, confident me said. But it didn't mean my curiosity had died. I still wanted to know what Nichelle had in her cooler and why Lucas needed it.

I managed to shove it all aside and dig into the new cookbook. For a change, this one was a straightforward book of recipes, all centered around eating better, using organic ingredients and whole foods. It was a movement that intrigued me; I liked the idea of locally grown vegetables and fresh baked bread, grain fed beef and happy chickens. At the same time, I didn't want anyone taking away my potato chips and onion dip. It was a balance.

Finally, I found a vegetable fricassee recipe that appealed to me. I tried to post a variety of food in my column, and I was about due for a non-meat dish. Most of the ingredients were ones I could get at the farmers' market just outside town, so I made a list, grabbed my purse and headed to the car.

Just as I stepped out the front door, a sleek blue Thunderbird purred to the curb in front of the house next to mine. I stood frozen as I watched a petite woman with nearly white-blonde hair emerge and walk toward Lucas's front door. She wore large sunglasses on her small face, and she moved with purpose and precision. Her black skirt ended several inches above her knees, and even though it was close to ninety degrees, she'd paired the skirt with a matching unstructured jacket that swung around her slim hips. I would've been drenched with sweat, but she looked as though she'd just stepped out of the frozen foods section.

Although I hadn't gotten a good look at her face, my impression was that she couldn't have been more than twenty-five. Something akin to jealousy sizzled in my gut.

I didn't move as she rang the doorbell. Within seconds, Lucas opened the door and stepped onto the porch. I heard his voice rise in what sounded like glad welcome, and after the barest of hesitations, he hugged her.

It could be his sister. Or his niece, even. Or a cousin. An old friend. An ex-lover.

Lucas stood aside, holding out his arm to let the girl go into the house ahead of him. He followed, but before he did, he glanced in my direction, at my house. If he saw me standing in the shadows of my porch, he didn't give any indication before he went inside.

Once he was out of sight, I finally unfroze. Stomping down to my practical silver sedan, the complete opposite of the dream machine parked at my neighbor's house, I climbed in and slammed the door.

I drove on autopilot all the way to the Drummond farm. It had stung to see Lucas greeting the gorgeous young blonde, more than it should have. I reminded myself that I'd only met this man two days before. I didn't know him. Anything I'd felt for him was imagined. It meant nothing.

"It's your pride that's hurt," I muttered as I pulled into the farm stand. "And your crazy imagination. This kind of thing doesn't happen in real life. It's not all perfect meet-cutes and happily-ever-afters. Pull up your damned big girl pants and get over it."

Strong, confident me was sulking about the whole deal, which only left mad and hurt me to skulk around the stand, picking up celery, onions and carrots. The citrus looked good, so I added some oranges and lemons to the basket over my arm. I absently squeezed a few eggplant and avocados before adding them, too. Damn him, he'd made me think about what was possible, when for so long, I'd been perfectly content to just exist.

And if I were honest with myself, I had to admit that the age deal was part of the sting. I didn't have hang-ups about being over thirty. I was cool with it. My twenties had been fraught with drama and angst and anxiety, trying to establish my career. Then had come the train wreck that was Will Harmon. Turning thirty and putting all of that behind me had been a relief. But while I thought I looked pretty damn good for my age, no way I could pull off young and dewy, if that was what Lucas was looking for in a woman.

Mrs. Drummond smiled at me as I brought up my basket of veggies to pay. "Still dang hot, isn't it? Doesn't feel like fall."

I nodded. "True. No changing leaves, no frost on the pump-kins."

She frowned as she examined one of the eggplants I'd se-lected. "This one seems like it's bruised. There's some soft spots right here." She pointed to one side of the purple flesh.

I winced a little. Yeah, I might've gripped the veggies a lit-tle too tight while I raged around the stand. The poor defenseless eggplant had never hurt anyone.

Mrs. Drummond set it aside. "Why don't you go get another one?"

I reached for the eggplant and put it back in my basket. "No, it's okay. I like this one. The bruises won't matter, because I'm making fricassee. I'll just cut around them." I pasted on a smile. "That's the beauty of a fricassee. You can use veggies that aren't perfect."

She shrugged. "Suit yourself."

After I paid and began to drive home, yesterday's dialogue ran through my head on a loop.

You're funny and interesting, and of course you're damned beautiful.

I don't think it's safe to get you involved. . .

But it was okay for Blondie to get involved. To get a hug. To be invited into his house. Maybe she was more *damned beautiful* than me and maybe she was younger than me, too. A thought struck me: he was a college professor. Was Blondie a student? Had they met when he taught her, and had they been together as more than teacher and pupil?

I turned into Golden Rays, waved at Mrs. Nelson, who was sweeping her walk, and then at Mr. Sullivan, who was walking his mean-ass little yippy dog. I rounded the corner to my block and skidded into my driveway. The powder blue Thunderbird was still parked there on the curb where it'd been when I left. Seeing the car gave me another surge of irrational irritation and hurt.

I threw the gearshift into park, undid my seat belt and twisted to the back seat. I snagged one of the canvas bags and yanked it up to my shoulder. Before any part of me could talk myself out of it, I got out of the car and strode to Lucas's front door.

The doorbell was under my finger before I stopped to think. I heard voices inside, muffled, and then footsteps approached. Lucas opened the door, frowning down at me in surprise.

"Jackie. What're you doing here?" There was strain in his voice and a modicum of impatience. He leaned against the door, the muscles in his arms tensed.

"I. . ." All the adrenaline that had carried me over here evaporated. "I had to go to the farmers' market this morning for ingredients. And they had oranges they'd just picked. So I thought you might want some." I slid the bag off my shoulder. "Here. You could. . .well, you could juice them, if you have a juicer. Or even if not, you can squeeze them by hand. Or just eat them. They're really sweet and juicy this season."

Lucas stared at the bag and then looked back at me. "Oranges?"

"Yeah." I swallowed. "You know. Florida oranges."

Heels clicked on the tile, and Blondie ducked under Lucas's arm. Huge ice blue eyes swept down me and then rose to rest on my face. She didn't smile or frown, only maintained a carefully neutral expression, watchful and cool.

"Lucas. Aren't you going to introduce me?" Her voice was low and even.

His jaw clenched. "Cathryn, I don't really think this is a good idea."

"Don't be silly." Those perfect lips curved into a smile. "Come in, won't you? Did I hear you brought Lucas oranges? How nice of you. And you're right, they're especially good this year."

Lucas exhaled. "Fine." He stood back, and I stepped into the house. The shutter blinds on the windows were all closed against the afternoon sunlight, so it almost appeared to be twilight. I'd expected boxes and chaos, but the furniture was arranged, and there were even a few pictures hung on the wall. I guessed I knew now how Lucas had been occupying his time.

Cathryn sat down in an overstuffed wing chair, while Lucas and I both perched on the edge of the brown sofa. Lucas pointed at me. "Cathryn, this is Jackie O'Brien. She's my next-door neighbor. Jackie, Cathryn Whitmore. She's. . ." His voice trailed off. "An old friend."

One corner of Cathryn's mouth quirked just slightly, which told me there was more to them than friends. "I'm glad to meet you, Jackie. Forgive me for being blunt, but aren't you a little young for this neighborhood?"

I nodded. "Yeah, I bring down the average, I guess. I lived with my grandmother while she was ill, and she left me the house after. . .well, after."

"I'm sorry for your loss." Cathryn sounded genuinely regretful. "That's something you and Lucas have in common. Did you know his aunt?"

"I did. Ellen. . .she kept to herself, mostly. But when I did talk to her, she seemed like a lovely woman."

"She was very shy." Lucas startled me, speaking up. "But she was kind. I didn't know her very well, but I came down here to visit her a while back."

I cocked my head. "That must've been before I moved in with Nana. I don't remember seeing you."

His forehead wrinkled. "It was. . .six years ago, I think. Your grandmother was a red-headed Irish lady? I met her. She was cool." We looked at each other for a few minutes, as I absorbed that fact. He'd met Nana.

With no little effort, I turned back to Cathryn. "Do you live around here, or are you just visiting?"

She smiled. "I live about an hour or so northwest of here. I'm a Florida native, for several generations. I met Lucas this summer when we were both vacationing in Cape May, and he told me he was moving to my neck of the woods. I just came down. . .to visit."

Visit or booty call? The bitchy thought floated through my mind before I could squelch it. I caught a flicker of something in Cathryn's eye. . .amusement? Discomfort? I knew I tended to show everything I thought on my face, and I concentrated on putting on a pleasant expression that was as blank as hers. I needed to get out, and now, before I blurted something I'd regret.

"Well, don't let me interrupt your, um, visit." I stood up and scooted between Lucas and the coffee table, looking for the quickest route to the door. My flip-flop wedged beneath the bottom of his shoe, and before I could catch myself, I launched forward, landing on top of him, between his legs, with my hands on his shoulders.

Lucas's fingers went to my waist to keep me from falling further. "Are you okay?"

"Yes." I ground out the word, frustrated and embarrassed. Why the hell couldn't I manage to stay on my feet in front of this guy? The warmth of his hands seared through my shirt and shorts, making me acutely aware of how close I was to him. If I leaned just a fraction of an inch closer, my lips could be—

Across the room, Cathryn cleared her throat. "Lucas, help her up. For heaven's sake, don't just sit there."

I pushed up against his shoulders and straightened. "I'm fine. Sorry about that." I waved off their concern. "I just—well, have a good visit. Enjoy the oranges. I won't bother you while you. . .catch up." I made it to the door without stumbling again, by the grace of whatever was holy. I heard Lucas calling me as I walked blindly across the yard, but I didn't turn my head or stop until I reached the safety of my own house.

Humiliation must have been exhausting, because once home,

I crawled into my bed, buried my face in the pillow and fell asleep, escaping from the memory of how I'd just made a fool of myself again. . .and this time, in front of a whole new audience.

It was early evening by the time I woke up. I blinked into the gray light filtering in through the blinds, feeling disoriented and trying to remember why I'd been so upset. As it all came back to me, I remembered that I'd left the vegetables from the farmers' market in my car. My car, which was parked in the heat of the Florida sun. Groaning, I rolled over. This day had been a disaster.

I got up, washed my face and ventured to peek out the blinds. Cathryn's Thunderbird was gone, and there wasn't any movement from Lucas's direction. I snuck out to the car and retrieved my bags as fast and quietly as I could. To my relief, the produce wasn't a total loss. I was able to save it, even if some of the leaves were a little wilted. I put the celery in water to revive it and stuck everything else in the fridge.

Warmed coq au vin made me a decent dinner. I forced it down along with a glass of Pinot Grigio and washed the dishes in the silence broken only by the click of Makani's nails against the tile as he searched for any bit of food I might've dropped on the floor. The temperature had gone down dramatically after sunset, and a lovely breeze rustled the leaves outside. I turned off my porch light to keep the bugs away and ventured out to sit in the dark with my second glass of wine, curled up in the rocking chair in the corner.

Rocking gently, I lay my head against the wooden back of the chair and closed my eyes. My shoulders relaxed as I began to feel the effects of the wine wash away the lingering pain of the day. The wind stirred my hair over my face, and I didn't move to brush it off.

"It's a beautiful night."

My heart jumped at the sound of Lucas's voice just below me. I didn't open my eyes or stop rocking as I swallowed down my surprise.

"It is." I didn't trust myself to say much more.

I heard the creak as he sank on to the step. For a few minutes, we were both silent. When Lucas spoke again, it was soft, almost part of the breeze itself.

"Jackie, I'm sorry about everything. If I've been. . .odd. You've been kind to me, and I'm sure I've come off like a dick. At least, that's what Cathryn says."

A chill fell over me at the mention of her name. "She's very pretty."

"Yeah, she is." He paused, and I heard him take a deep breath. "She's one of the most amazing people I've ever met. We stayed at the same bed and breakfast this summer, in Cape May, and we had a little adventure. I thought. . .for a while, I thought we might have something together. Something real. And I thought that she felt the same way." He laughed a little, a short humorless cough. "I know what you're thinking. She's a lot younger than me. But Cathryn's older than she looks. I mean, yeah, she's twenty-five, but she's an old soul."

"I knew it." Satisfaction tinged my voice, and I let my eyes drift open a little to watch Lucas.

"What did you know?" He shifted so his back was against the railing.

"That she was twenty-five. I thought that when I saw her this morning." I brought my knees up and wrapped my arms around them. "What happened? I mean, between the two of you. If you don't mind me asking."

Lucas raised one eyebrow. "I wish I knew. She called me about two weeks before I moved, and she said it wasn't going to work between us. I guess it turned out to be just a summer fling to her. She wants to be friends, which is cool. I called her as soon as I got down here."

"I'm sorry." Disappointment flooded my heart. He was still in love with her. I'd been hoping he'd say the break-up had been his idea. But if Cathryn had broken his heart, he might still be pining for her. "That must be hard on you."

"Ah, well. . .I don't know. Maybe we didn't have much in common. We bonded over what happened to us, and it might've turned out that was all it was."

"Can I ask what the adventure was? Or is that private?"

"I really shouldn't. . .well, okay." He looked at me, his eyes speculative. "You'll probably think I'm insane, though."

When I stared back, my gaze steady, he laughed.

"Too late, huh? Yeah, I guess so. May as well just spill it, then." He leaned back, and the muscles in his arms stood out, making my mouth suddenly dry. His gray cotton shirt fit snugly over his abs. It had ridden up just a little so I could see the top of his jeans, which rode low on his hips. I was abruptly and almost painfully aware of the subtle strength of his body. With difficulty, I brought my attention back to what he was saying.

"We both stayed at an old B and B right on the beach. It turned out that it was haunted. And our rooms were particularly affected. We worked together to help the spirits find rest."

My mouth fell open. When I could find my voice, it was hollow. "All you had to say was that it was private. You didn't have to make something up."

Lucas laughed. "Yeah, I know. It sounds like a lie. But that's really what happened. It's how we met. I swear to you, I know it seems nuts, but that's honestly the true story." He gazed out into the night. "There's more out there in the world than what anyone guesses."

I took a few minutes to absorb it. "What was wrong with the spirits? What did you have to do help them? Like. . .exorcism?"

"Uh. . ." Lucas licked his lips and looked down at his hands. I sensed his embarrassment. "They were two young lovers. They had died violently, before their love was, um, consummated. And we helped them find peace."

A smile curved my lips. "Why, Lucas, are you blushing?"

He shook his head. "Of course not. I just—it sounds so weird, saying it out loud to someone who didn't experience it."

"It does, to be honest. But for some reason, I don't doubt

your sanity. You just said it so matter-of-factly, I believe you."

He grinned at me, and I could just make out his dimple in the moonlight. "Thanks. I think."

We sat in companionable silence for a few minutes, with only the rhythmic creak of my rocking chair and the sound of cicadas surrounding us.

"Lucas." I spoke just above a whisper. "If you can tell me about your ghost story, why can't you tell me what's going on with you now? It can't be any worse than that."

He dropped his head back against the post, closing his eyes. "I wish I could say you're right. It's not that I don't want to tell you. Believe me, I'm feeling very much alone in this. If it weren't for Cathryn, I'd be stark raving mad."

I stopped rocking and slid from the chair, scooting until I sat on the step, too, just inches from Lucas. He watched me with trepidation.

"You don't know me. I get that. But I'm a good listener. I don't judge and I don't offer advice that isn't wanted. So just know that I'd be happy to be a sounding board, if you need one."

"Thank you." He reached across and covered my hand with his. "I'll keep that in mind."

We were quiet for a few minutes. I gazed out into the night, hyper-aware of Lucas's fingers over mine, the touch of his skin. I was afraid to speak or to move, lest I might break this spell.

"You told Cathryn that you moved down here when your grandmother was ill. Where did you live before? And how long have you been writing your column?"

I smiled. "So we're talking about me now, is that it?"

Lucas laughed. "I was hoping I'd made the transition smooth enough that you wouldn't notice."

"Hard to get anything by me. But okay. I lived in New York. I was born and grew up in a small town on the Hudson River." I closed my eyes, picturing home. "I went to school for journalism, but cooking was always my passion. I worked at the magazine right out of college, and I'd just gotten the column assignment when Nana got sick. It was okay with my bosses for me to work from home, whether that was New York or Florida, so here I am."

He nodded. "Not a lot of people would give up their own lives to take care of a sick grandparent. What about your parents?"

I shook my head. "My mom and dad would've dropped everything to come down, but I wanted to do it. Nana pretty much raised us—that's my brothers and me, I mean. My parents are awesome, but they both have demanding jobs, so Nana was the one who packed my lunches, kissed my boo-boos and let me play hooky from school on the opening day of our favorite movies. It wasn't even an option for me not to be there for her."

"What do your parents do?"

"My mom owns a small regional newspaper. She's transitioned it to a monthly with a daily e-copy, and that's how it's survived in the cyber age. My dad's a chef, and he owns his own restaurant."

Lucas grinned. "So your mom writes and your dad cooks. And you. . .write a cooking column. There's some kind of psychological thing there, right? Like you're a blend of them both?"

"Oh, you've figured me out." I rolled my eyes. "Yeah, I know. It's crazy. But it's in our blood. My brother Tim works for Mom's paper, and Bret opened his own restaurant two years ago. Neither of them planned to do it—Tim went to law school—but here we are. Products of our upbringing."

"Do you like what you do?" Lucas still hadn't let go of my hand, which made me very happy even though my arm was beginning to cramp from keeping it still.

"Hmmm? Oh. . .mostly. I did when I started out, but by now, it's getting a little old. I cook these recipes and think how much better I could do it."

He chuckled. "I bet. I felt the same way as a professor, giving my students reading assignments. So why don't you quit and write your own cookbook?"

I shrugged. "I've considered it, but I like my income from the magazine, and I'm not sure I've found my unique niche for a cookbook. I think it's got to be something special. I don't want to write another book about cooking on a budget or with whole foods. . .it's been done."

"I understand." Lucas regarded me, with his mouth twisted. "What kind of restaurant does your dad own?"

I smiled. "It's like everything else in our family: a mix of all of us. My mom is fully Italian. Her parents were born in Italy. My dad's mom—that's Nana—was born here in the US, but her parents both came over from County Cork. So Dad does a mash-up of Irish and Italian dishes."

"That sounds amazing. What's the name of the restaurant?"

Shaking my head, I pulled my hand away at last and covered my face. "It's so corny. But they came up with it before I was born, so I take no responsibility for this. It's called A Bit O'Rome."

"I love it. I get the corny, but since it's not my family, I think it's funny. I'd love to see it."

A pang of hope made my heart stutter. "Maybe someday."

Lucas licked his lips, and watching his tongue, a thrill of need shot through my core as he spoke.

"Maybe someday."

"Lucas. Don't stop. *Don't stop.*" I moaned the words and clutched at his hands between my legs.

"Never." His fingers moved over me, and I knew I was on the edge, ready to plunge into ecstasy. And then he licked my nose with a cold, wet tongue.

I blinked into the early morning light and focused on the

expectant face of Makani. I'd given in last night to his soulful don't-crate-me-eyes and let him sleep on the bed with me again. My reward was the interruption of one of my increasingly-regular Lucas-centric sex dreams.

"We've got to stop meeting like this." I tucked the puppy between my arm and my body and pulled him in for a snuggle. "You're ruining some very interesting dreams lately." He cocked his head, his small face quizzical.

Burying my face in the pillow, I sighed and pushed myself up. Things between Lucas and me were moving along. . .but they hadn't yet reached the point of my dreams, which was a shame, because these dreams sizzled.

Big news was short-lived in our community, and within a few days of it happening, the excitement of Lucas moving in and my own spectacular blunders had faded from the gossip circuit. Mrs. Mac was in the midst of planning her next block soiree, there was a cheating scandal in the canasta club and Mrs. Walters, widowed for several decades, had been spotted sneaking out of Mr. Carlton's house in the wee hours of the morning. Lucas and I were yesterday's headlines.

A week after Cathryn's visit, I finally gave in to Al's repeated suggestions and summoned enough courage to ask Lucas to have dinner with me at Leone's.

"Can we eat early?" He looked so serious, so sexy professor, sitting on the step of my porch, wearing his gold-rimmed glasses. Most of the time, I'd learned, he wore contact lenses, but sometimes, by the time he joined me in the evenings, after a long day of working on his book, he'd already taken them out for the night. And each time he did, it made me want to kiss him until those glasses steamed up.

"Early?" I tried to bring my attention back to his words and ignore the mouth saying them. "Um, sure."

He grinned, making that irresistible dimple pop out. "Maybe Mrs. Mac and company are beginning to rub off on me. Pretty soon I'll be eating breakfast at four, lunch at ten and dinner at three."

"Well, it can be tempting to fall into the rhythms around here. But in this case, I think we can make it work. Al and I've started working on his cookbook. So why don't we have a late lunch/early dinner deal, and I can show him my notes at the same time?"

And that was how I found myself sitting shotgun in Lucas's car as he drove us the few blocks to Leone's the next afternoon. His knuckles were tight on the steering wheel, and his lips were set in a tight line.

"Hey, are you okay?" I touched his arm.

"Yeah. I'm just not much on crowds lately. Or driving."

I bit back a sigh. "Crowds won't be an issue at Leone's, not this time of day. And I could've driven. You just had to tell me."

"I'll be okay." He slid me a glance. "So you and the owner of the diner are friends?"

"Yes. Actually more like family by this time. When Nana came down here, she was a little homesick, and she just happened into this restaurant. Al made her the food she was used to eating with my mom and our family. He'd moved down here ten years before, after his wife died, and I think he was lonely. He and Nana became friends. When I moved down to take of her, after the stroke, he brought me food to the hospital, and then to the house. He used to stop by on his way home, just to check on us." I closed my eyes, remembering. "We thought she was getting better, but she made me promise that if she had another stroke, I'd let her go. When it happened, my mom and dad and my brothers couldn't get down here fast enough. Al didn't want me to go through it alone, so he stayed with Mrs. Mac and me that night. He was with us when she died."

Lucas smiled. "He sounds like a good man."

"He is." I nodded as we turned into the diner parking lot. "I tell him all the time, if he were fifty years younger, I'd want him for my boyfriend."

"Ah, so I'm about to meet the competition?" Lucas raised

his eyebrows, and my heart sped up. More and more often, he'd been making the occasional comment that tempted me to think he was interested in me as more than a friend. In us. I tried not to put too much stock in those teases, since most of the time he followed up by pulling back fast.

"No competition." I tossed him a saucy look. "Al will always have my heart."

Watching the two men size up each other that afternoon was amusing. For the first thirty minutes, they circled around in wariness. But when they discovered a shared passion for the history and mythology of ancient Rome, it was as though they were lifelong friends.

"This boy, he's not so bad." Al patted my shoulder when Lucas had excused himself to use the men's room. "A shame he's not Italian, huh?"

"No, but he's Irish, so Nana would've liked that."

"Maybe." Al rubbed one finger over his bristly chin. "You don't think he's hiding anything from you anymore? No more mafia questions?"

I shrugged. "I don't think I know everything about the guy, no. I think. . .there's still more going on than he's telling me. But I've decided that I can wait until he's ready to share."

"Good thinking." Al nodded. "And I don't think you were on the right path, anyway. I reached out to a few people after you asked me, and no one had heard talk of any witnesses on the run."

"Thanks for checking, Al. I appreciate it. Chalk it up to my overactive imagination." I pulled a tablet from my bag. "Here're the notes we talked about for the cookbook. I took the list of recipes we discussed and narrowed down our focus. We'll need to start planning out each dish, and as we discussed, for book-quality pictures, we need to hire a professional photographer. Look this over, and we'll finalize everything next week."

Al's face broke into a smile. "Excellent. I called my children last Sunday and told them all about it, and now everyone wants to tell me which of their favorites must be included."

I laughed. "Then you have your work cut out for you, my friend!"

On the way home, Lucas was quiet. "I like him. But I see what you mean. No competition, is there? I'm beat."

"I'm afraid so. If Al says the word, I'm his. I can see the day coming when I convince him to run off to the Italian Riviera with me. Just you watch."

Lucas smiled, but there was sadness in his eyes. "Jackie. . ." He began to speak and then lapsed into silence. "Never mind."

I wasn't sure why, but I didn't see Lucas for several days after that.

Despite the fact that we were spending more time together, I wasn't any closer to discovering Lucas's secrets. He continued to stay in his house most of the time, and as the weeks went by, I got into the habit of glancing out the window, checking to see if he were coming or going. I spotted Nichelle making deliveries every few days. Lucas didn't mention her when we spoke, and neither did I.

He came to visit me most evenings if I sat out on my porch. I invited him inside a few times, but he always declined. We talked for hours about books, plays, movies and music. And while I loved our conversations, I was always aware that we never touched on anything important or too personal.

"Billy Joel is the voice of our generation." Lucas was sprawled on the floor of the porch, leaning against the house as he pointed at me. "His music tells our stories. How can you not see that?"

"It's not that I don't like him." I shrugged. "But I like Elton John, too. And Bruce Springsteen. James Taylor. And what about Carol King? You can't say that *Tapestry* wasn't one of the best albums ever produced." I quirked one eyebrow. "And you do realize we're seriously dating ourselves by talking about stuff that came out when we were infants. Or not even born yet."

"But it's—" He stopped suddenly, and the same odd expression I'd seen a few times before crossed his face. As always, he jumped to his feet. "I'm sorry, Jackie. I have to go."

He was down the steps and half way back home before I could struggle out of my chair. I leaned around the house, straining to see him as he ran up the steps of the deck to his back door. I watched to see lights flicker on, but the house remained dark. I knew his car was parked in the driveway on the opposite side. As far as I could see, it never moved.

I sat down again with a deep sigh. Every time I thought Lucas was beginning to relax and trust me, he seemed to draw back again. I didn't know if it was something I was doing or failing to do, but I was getting tired of the entire situation.

Through the open window, I heard the trill of my cell phone ringing. I jumped up to grab it, wondering if it might be Lucas, calling with an explanation. He'd agreed to take my number in case of emergency, but he'd yet to use it. Of course, I hadn't called him yet either, though his info was logged into my contacts.

And tonight wasn't going to be any different. Leesa's name flashed across the screen.

"Hey, Leese." I dropped onto the sofa.

"Hi there, chickadee. I'm calling for an update on the boy-next-door."

I rolled my eyes. "Leesa, honestly. There's nothing to tell. Nothing's going on." If I sounded a little disgruntled by that fact, I couldn't help it. The more time I spent around Lucas, the more I liked him. And the more it bothered me that a secret stood between us.

"Honey, from where I sit, this is the kind of situation where you're going to have to make the first move. And I think it's about time."

"Hmm. Where *you* sit, my dear, is a thousand miles away in New York. You have no idea. Maybe he's not at all interested in me."

"And why does that matter? I hear it your voice, Jacks.

66

You're hot for his bod. When you spent ten minutes the other night telling me about his forearms, I knew you had it bad. Jump his bones, girlfriend. Make it happen."

"Maybe he doesn't want me to jump his bones. Maybe he doesn't like me that way."

"Bullshit. They all want it. He might not want a long-term hookup, but he's a man. You offer him the goods, he's going to say yes. And if he doesn't, you can be sure he plays for the other team. Not that there's anything wrong with that, but I'm telling you, sweetie, any guy who turns you down isn't interested in girls."

I sighed. "I hear you, Leese, He's still doing the disappearing act, though. Tonight he was in the middle of telling me how great Billy Joel is, and suddenly he gets this look on his face, and before I can get out a word, he's gone. Like a flash across the yard. Whoosh."

Leesa didn't speak for a minute. "Jacks, did you ever think. . .maybe he's a superhero?"

I gritted my teeth. "Come on, Leesa. Be serious."

"I am, I totally am. What if he's getting the call? You know, like Batman seeing the signal? Or Spiderman with his Spidey sense?"

"Okay, sure. I live next door to a superhero. That's the secret. You know, come to think of it, that's the second time you've mentioned Spidey lately. What's up with you?"

I heard her sigh. "I didn't want to tell you this, but. . .I'm seeing someone. And he's totally obsessed with comic books, particularly Spiderman. I guess it's rubbing off on me."

I squealed, wriggling on the couch. "Leesa! Why didn't you tell me? I'm so happy for you! What's he like? What's his name?"

"I didn't tell you because I didn't want the third degree. And because I wasn't sure. . .I wasn't sure how it was going to stick. But he seems to like me, and God, Jacks, he's like nerd-sexy. His name is Harold. You might not look at him twice if you passed him on the street, but when we're together, he gives me his complete attention. And let me tell you. . .in bed, he gives me his *total* attention. And the boy does his homework."

I fanned myself with my hand. "Stop. I'm about to combust. Leese, I'm so glad. It almost makes me want to fly up there and meet him."

"You totally should. I have to confess, I told him all about you and Lucas, and the whole Spiderman scenario was his idea. He'd love to meet you both."

"Some day, maybe. For now. . .tell me more about your sexy nerd lover. I'm completely jealous."

Since Leesa was not one to spare details, I spent the next hour hearing all the blush-inducing juicy stories. By the time we hung up, I'd finished my second beer of the night and was seriously in need of some attention myself.

I dropped the phone onto an end table and lay back, closing my eyes. My dreams of Lucas had amped up the heat lately, making it harder to be around him during our porch evenings. I wanted his hands on me. I wanted to touch his chest, run my hands down those tight abs and see where they took me.

Sitting up, I peered out the window into the dark, looking for any clue that Lucas was still inside his house, awake. The alcohol made me bold enough to slide my feet into flip-flops, grab another two beers and venture across the yard.

I climbed up to the deck and knocked on the back door. My heart began to pound a little faster, whether it was in anticipation of what might happen—hot damn—or from nerves that I was actually doing this.

I didn't hear anything at first. I began to think Leesa was right: he was a super-hero, and he was still out on some risky mission, not knowing I was here at his door, ready to offer him—

"Jackie?" The door swung open, and Lucas stood before me, his eyes bleary and confused. "What are you doing here? It's nearly midnight."

"Yeah, I know. I just. . ." I swallowed hard. Now that he

was right in front of me, I was about to lose my nerve. I thought about Leesa and Harold and plunged ahead. "You had to leave so suddenly. I brought over a couple of beers for us to drink. Can I come in?"

He glanced over my shoulder, all around us, and then down at me. Caution warred with some other compelling emotion on his face until he stepped back. "Of course."

Only one dim light burned in the kitchen. I set the two bottles of beer on the table and turned to face him. "Did I wake you up?"

"No, I just got back." His eyes widened, as if he realized he'd said more than he'd intended.

"Where did you go?" I pulled out a chair and sat down, twisting the top of one of the beers. "When you practically sprinted off my porch a few hours ago, I mean."

Lucas regarded me solemnly before he joined me at the table. He opened his beer and took a long pull. "I can't tell you, Jackie. I'm sorry."

I kept my eyes on his, steady and serious. "Okay. But can I ask you one more question?"

"You can ask. I can't promise I'll answer."

"Are you a superhero?"

Lucas choked on his beer, coughing and sputtering as he set it down. "What? Am I a *what?*"

I smiled. "A superhero. I mean, look at the evidence." I held up my fingers. "You're secretive about who you are and what you do. You take off suddenly, and you can't tell me why. You have this chick making some kind of mysterious deliveries to you. That all adds up to superhero."

He shook his head. "You've been reading too many comics. No, Jackie, I promise you. I'm not a superhero. I wish that were it."

"Then what? I don't understand why you can't at least give me a clue. I've been trying to give you space. Let you tell me in your own time. But it's getting old, Lucas."

He rubbed the back of his neck. "I know. You've been patient. You don't know how many times I've wanted to just tell you. We sit in the dark together night after night, and each time, it's harder for me to stop myself from spilling my guts. Mostly because I know if I did, you might end up hating me. And I'm selfish enough that I can't take that chance. Because as difficult as it is to keep my secret. . ." He raised his eyes to meet mine. "It's even harder to harder to keep myself from touching you."

I took another swig of my beer and set it down. Taking a deep breath, I stood up and stepped closer to the chair where Lucas watched me with hooded eyes. I slid my arms around his neck and brought my lips close to his ear.

"I could never hate you, Lucas. I want you to touch me. I want *you.*"

Straddling his chair, I sat down on his lap and trailed my mouth down his neck. His skin was an intoxicating mix of salt and lime, making me think of a margarita. I let my tongue dart out, tracing circles on his skin.

Lucas groaned. His hands gripped my hips, pulling me closer to him. "Jackie. . ." He turned his head just in time to meet my lips with his as I raised my chin from his throat.

There was no hesitation. Every worry I'd had about him rejecting me vanished as his mouth consumed me. One hand shot up to the back of my neck, holding me in place as his lips stroked, sucked and caressed. I pressed my breasts against him, wanting more, suffocated by a longing unlike any I'd ever known.

I reached between us, all thoughts of finesse gone. I only wanted, wanted now. My fingers fumbled at the button of his jeans.

"Jackie." Lucas dragged his mouth away from me. His eyes were wide and frantic. "You've got to stop. I don't know if— you've got to stop now. You have to step back. I can't, but you have to. Please."

"Why?" I plunged my hands under his shirt, running them over his chest, around to his back. "Stopping is the last thing I want to do. I want you, Lucas. I want you now. Don't ask me to stop."

"*Jackie*." This time he sounded desperate. "Do it. Get off me. Or—I might hurt you."

I froze. His words cut through my happy beer haze, through the beat of my desire. Slowly I slid off his lap, pressing my hands to my face as I stared down at him.

Lucas brought his hand to his forehead, squeezing as though he was holding in a killer headache.

"What the hell do you mean?" I could barely manage the whisper. "You might hurt me? Are you. . .are you threatening me?"

"God, Jackie, no. I don't want to hurt you." He reached over and took my hand, bringing it to his lips. "Please. I want this—I want *you*—as much as you do. But I'm scared. Who I am now—what I am—I could do something and not even be aware of it. The last thing I want to do is turn you away. But I don't know what might happen. And I can't ask you to trust me when I haven't even told you the truth."

"What're you talking about? What you are now? What do you mean by that?"

Lucas's eyes were nearly black. "I can't tell you."

All of my control dissolved in an explosion of temper and want. "Fuck that, Lucas. Yes, you can. Tell me. What the hell is wrong with you?"

He jumped to his feet and stalked across the kitchen, putting distance between us. "You won't believe me even if I do tell you."

I snorted. "I just asked if you were a superhero. Are you kidding me? Tell me. At this point, I'm not sure there's anything you could say that I wouldn't buy."

Lucas ran his hand over his face and gripped the edge of the counter. His chest was rising and falling rapidly as he breathed. "Promise me you won't take off. Promise me you'll hear me out."

I nodded, slowly sinking back into my chair. "I promise."

He stared at me, and when he spoke, his voice was low, even as his words carried to me with perfect clarity.

"I think. . .I'm pretty sure. . ." He sucked in another breath. "I'm a vampire, Jackie."

Chapter 5

WHEN I WAS eleven years old, I took a dare from Joshua Kreely about how long I could hold onto the merry-go-round on the school playground. I gripped the cold metal pipes that made up the handles as three big boys used their shoulders to make the turntable spin faster and harder than any of us had ever seen it move.

For the first few minutes, I held tight, confident and strong. But after a little while, my stomach began to turn, my palms began to sweat, and my head pounded. It became harder to keep my grip. Finally, the world began to look hazy around its edges, and before I knew it, I'd loosened my hold and was flying across the gravel and macadam that made up our schoolyard.

I landed in grass, which was fairly miraculous, given how little soft ground there was near the play area. But when I hit the ground, I had the breath knocked out of me, and for several terrifying moments, I couldn't take in any oxygen. Leesa later told me my mouth opened and closed like a fish on the beach, and my eyes were huge and frightened. Though the whole episode wasn't very long, for me it felt like an eternity.

When the words Lucas had spoken filtered through my brain, I felt the same way. I'd gone flying across the yard and landed on hard ground. I couldn't find my breath.

When my vision cleared, Lucas was still across the kitchen, his eyes fastened on me.

"Are you okay?"

I stood up and took one shaky step back. "What do you think? Are you out of your fucking mind? Or are you—" A sob tore out of my throat. "Are you trying to get rid of me? Did you think up the most implausible story you could, just to make me leave you alone? I thought we were friends, at least. All you had to say was, 'Jackie, I don't feel the same way about you.'"

"That's not it. I told you it was going to sound crazy. I said you wouldn't believe me." He clenched his jaw and growled. "I don't know how to prove it to you. Or even if I should."

I paused for a second. "You're serious. You really think you're a-a vampire."

He blinked once and then nodded. "I think so. I don't know for sure. Something happened to me right before I came down here. There's other stuff, too. It's complicated. I told you, my life is totally fucked up right now. But you wanted to know. And now you do."

Gripping the chair, I pulled it closer to me, further from Lucas, and sat down. I wasn't sure my legs were going to hold me up any longer. I reached for my beer and took a big sip. I needed it.

"Tell me what happened. What makes you think—oh my God, have you killed people? Drunk their blood?"

"No." Lucas approached the table slowly, careful not to spook me. "I haven't. Not from people." He cast his eyes down. "It's a long story."

"I have nothing but time."

The side of his mouth lifted. "Okay." He spread out his fingers on the table and stared down at them. "It started the night

I went out with some of my friends from Birch before I left. It was supposed to be my good-bye party. We went to a bar, and at first, it was fun. We drank, probably too much. And we got to doing shots, and then there was this woman. Her name, I think, was Veronica. She reminded me of, um, Cathryn." He flashed me a sheepish look. "Things had ended with Cathryn by then, and I wasn't heartbroken, necessarily, but I was hurt, I guess. A little surprised. But I was drunk enough that this woman seemed like a good idea.

"I just barely remember her being there, and then the next thing I remember, I was waking up in my hotel room with the worst damn hangover I'd ever had. I didn't know what'd happened, but there was a note on the mirror, from Veronica. It didn't really explain anything, except that she had set up a delivery and she'd done something to change my destiny. . I don't know, it was very cryptic."

I licked my lips. "Can I read it?"

Lucas shook his head. "I gave it to Cathryn when she was here last week. She's doing some research, trying to find out what happened to me."

"Why Cathryn?" I was lost.

"Oh, sorry. Cathryn. . .this is sort of her line of work. It's kind of a secret, but she works with people who have special abilities. She has a lot of connections, so I figured she was the best person to help me."

Good God, they were all insane. "Okay. So go on."

Lucas closed his eyes. "You think I'm crazy. All right, I get that. Half the time I think I'm crazy, too. Well, I read the note, and then this guy came to my hotel room with a cooler. It was full of bags of blood. In the note, Veronica had said to follow my instinct, and when I saw it. . .I needed it. I ripped open a bag and drank it. And then I drank another. That's when I figured out I'm probably a vampire."

My stomach turned over. "You seriously drink blood? Like. . .how much?"

Lucas glanced away. "Two or three bags a day. It's delivered to me, and I drink it." He reached across the table, wincing when I shrunk back. "Jackie, I think I'm maybe only partly a vampire. Because I don't want to hurt most people. I can hear their blood. I can smell it. But I don't attack them. I don't have fangs."

I didn't know how to reply to that. My world was spinning way out of control. Part of me wanted to ask more questions, and part of me wanted to get the hell out of here.

"You said you don't want to hurt most people. Are there people. . .you do want to hurt?"

His eyes turned bleak. "Not until tonight. And I don't want to hurt you. But oh, God, Jackie, when you were touching me, all I could think about was tasting you. It was the first time I wanted blood that didn't come in bags. It scared the hell out of me. And let me tell you, after what I've been through in the last few months, I thought I was done being scared."

I stared at him, unable to answer. Everything Lucas had said spun through my mind, and my brain stuttered on one tiny, unimportant fact that suddenly seemed to make sense.

"So the garlic. That's why you don't like it anymore? Because you think you're a vampire?"

He lifted one shoulder, his forehead wrinkling. "I don't know about why, but I can't eat it since that night, and every time I even smell it, I feel a little nauseated."

I frowned. "All that food I made, you didn't really eat it?"

"No, of course I ate it. Why wouldn't I? I just avoided the garlic."

"Vampires don't eat food. You drink blood, you just told me that."

"I thought you didn't believe I'm a vampire. If you think I'm crazy, why does it bother you that I ate real food? Which I did, by the way. I ate it all."

"Because if you're going to have a delusion, you need to be consistent about it. I've seen you in the sunlight, you don't have fangs, you cast a reflection—there's no way you're a vampire.

I don't know what happened to you that night in New Jersey, but isn't it possible someone's playing a huge practical joke on you?"

Lucas rolled his eyes. "You don't think I've taken every aspect of this whole mess into consideration? What's delivered to me, what I drink. . .it's blood, Jackie. I know it is. And. . ." He looked away, and his Adam's apple bobbed when he swallowed. "There's more to it. More that I absolutely can't explain in any rational terms."

"Oh, okay. I see. Because being a vampire, that explains some of this in rational terms. That's perfectly logical."

He stood and walked back to the far side of the kitchen. "Jackie, you asked me. You wanted to know. You told me once that you're the kind of person who listens without judging or offering advice. I'm not sure what you call this, but it sure as feels like judgment to me."

I jumped up and followed him. "Judging you? That's what you think I'm doing? Are you out of your freaking mind? Wait, don't answer that. I already know."

He threw up his hands. "Fine, I'm nuts. I'm—" He broke off mid-sentence as his eyes got that same trapped, almost hunted look I'd seen earlier on my front porch. He took one step toward me and pointed toward the door. "You need to leave now. Please."

I cocked my head, disbelief washing over me. "What the hell, Lucas? You drop this vampire shit on me, and then you tell me to go away because I don't buy it right away?" I reached to touch his arm. "Come on. Let's sit down and talk about this. There's got to be a more realistic explanation—"

"Jackie, I can't talk about this right now. You've got to— just go." He thrust my hand away from him as a wild look took over his eyes. "You don't understand."

I gripped his wrist. "No, I'm not leaving you. Look, I'm sorry. I didn't mean to make you feel bad. I did pester you to tell me. I should've been more compassionate when you did."

"It's not that. It's—" His hand covered mine, crushing my fingers in a steel grip. "Oh, my God, Jackie. Hold on."

And just like that, I was back on the spinning merry-go-round, flying through the air, waiting to hit concrete and feel all my bones break into a million splintered pieces. My stomach lurched, and pain sliced through my head. I couldn't see anything, and my only awareness centered on the heat of Lucas's skin beneath my fingers and the pressure of his hand above mine. I was certain that if I lost that, I'd go careening off into space and time, lost forever in a loop of dark and confusion.

With a thump, my feet hit solid ground, and slowly I became aware again. The first sense to return was smell, and I breathed in a long, appreciative sniff of garlic, tomatoes and coffee. I blinked, trying to clear my vision. Lucas stood in front of me, and he used the arm I wasn't gripping to draw me into him and hold me tight.

"Are you okay?" The whisper drifted down to my ear, and I shivered. He rubbed his cheek over the top of my head, and I relaxed against him, needing the moment to settle.

And then panic overtook me, interrupting my second of bliss, and I smacked his shoulder. "What the fuck, Lucas? What did you do to me? Where are we, what happened—"

"What the hell is she doing here?" The unfamiliar voice cut through my temper tantrum, and I pushed back to see who was here with us. Wherever here was.

As soon as I looked around, I knew where we were. Leone's. It was dark, with only the dim security lights still on, but this place was like a second home to me. I recognized the counter and the booths, even in the unfamiliar stillness. Lucas and I were just inside the door, steps away from my familiar booth.

Two men stood on the other side of the counter. Both wore suits, and both exhibited similar expressions of surprise. The man I'd heard speak was blond, and his suit was gray. The other had dark brown hair and a blue suit.

Lucas draped his arm around my shoulder and pulled me to

his side. "Long story. She was with me when the call came, and it just happened. Let's get on with it so I can get her home."

The second man nodded. "Of course." He turned to the man who had spoken first. "After you?"

Man Number One laughed. "That's how you like it, isn't it? I lay out all the sins, all the crimes, and then you jump in and explain them away."

The other guy smiled. "Not at all. I was just trying to be courteous. I'd be more than happy to go before you." He swept one arm out in front of himself. "But we should let the broker have a look first, don't you think?"

The expression on his counterpart's face darkened. He rolled his eyes. "Son of a bitch."

Lucas ran his hand down my arm and slid his fingers between mine. He tugged me forward slightly, and sorrow fell over his eyes. "Jackie, I'm sorry. But I don't want to let go of you here, and I need to—to see."

I stumbled after him, my balance still off after our trip—or whatever the hell that was—and he led me around the counter to stand near the kitchen door. I followed his gaze down to the floor and cried out in alarm.

"No! Al—Lucas, it's Al. Do something, call the ambulance." I tried to pry my hand loose from Lucas's so I could drop to my knees, but he only gripped it tighter.

"Jackie, I'm sorry. It's too late. He's gone. I'm so sorry."

I sobbed and twisted, still trying to get away. "No, you don't know that! Do something, won't you? CPR or. . ." My cry trailed off as I saw the pool of blood underneath the body of my friend and the spread of crimson staining the front of his shirt. "What happened to him, Lucas?" I turned to face the two men who stood just beyond Al's head. "Why did you do this?"

"They didn't, Jackie." Lucas held my hand between both of his and stroked the back of it. "Not them."

"Can we get on with it?" The blond man shifted his weight to his other leg. "You're not my only appointment tonight."

"Give her a minute." Compassion filled the voice of Man Number Two. "She knew him."

"That's the operative word here. *Knew*. What happened to his physical body isn't germane now. He's out of her world. Time to see what his next stop's going to be." Man Number One stared just past Al, his eyes cold and accusing. I sensed by the intensity of his focus that he was seeing something I couldn't. "Shall we begin in childhood? Incident one. Hatred. Cardinal in nature, directed toward his father. Incident two. Theft. Venial—"

"Wait." The second man held up one hand. He smiled at Lucas. "Look."

Lucas was staring at the same spot as the blond guy. As I watched, a hum filled the air. My breath caught as Lucas's eyes changed. They glowed golden, with a warmth and depth that made me dizzy all over again. His lips curved into a smile, and when he spoke, his voice carried a timber I hadn't heard before.

"This soul is redeemed by Grace. There is no need for a recounting and Reckoning. He moves on to Paradise immediately." Lucas inclined his head, and a whoosh of air blew past us. A moment later, his eyes returned to normal. The diner seemed somehow emptier, though the four of us still stood exactly where we had.

"What happened?" I glanced from one of them to the other. "What was that?"

"The soul left." Brown-haired man seemed pleased by the outcome.

"Another waste of time." Blond guy shook his head. "I'll never understand why we have to go through the motions when it's a done deal."

"If we didn't, the idea of Grace would hold no weight. Besides, it's not for you or me to make these decisions."

I glanced from one of them to the other. "I don't get it." I looked up at Lucas. "Are you. . .the Angel of Death?"

The other two men laughed. There was more than a hint of scorn in blond man's humor.

Lucas's face remained serious. "No. I'm—" He cast a glance at them. "According to these people, I'm what's known as a death broker. I negotiate the movement of souls."

"Are you sure?" I persisted. "Because if you're the Angel of Death, you can do something. You can bring Al back. It's not his time. He wasn't meant to die now, and not like this." My breath hitched. "He's a good man. He's lived a good life. He should die in his bed, in peace. Why can't you fix this?"

"I'm not the freaking Angel of Death, Jackie." Lucas's tone was anguished. "There is no such thing. Or if there is, I haven't met him, which wouldn't surprise me since no one tells me anything."

I wasn't giving up yet. "Are you sure? In all the books, there's an Angel of Death. He takes the souls to wherever they go."

The man in the gray suit laughed, but it was an ugly sound, full of derision. "She was expecting a brooding guy with stormy eyes who whisks people off to the River Styx." He glanced Lucas up and down. "Instead she gets the absent-minded professor who doesn't know what the hell he's doing. Can you blame her for feeling a little let down?"

"That's not fair." Brown hair/blue suit sighed. "Lucas has had an unusual transition."

"That's one word for it." The other man's mouth twitched. "Are we finished here? I'd like to leave."

"Fine." Lucas motioned with his free hand. He still held onto me with the other. "Go. Everything here is complete."

Within the blink of an eye, both men were gone, and Lucas and I stood alone with Al's body.

I covered my face with one hand. "Lucas, what happened to him? Who did this?"

He shook his head. "I don't know, Jackie. I'm sorry, but that isn't part of. . ." He swept his arm over the whole scene. "This. What I do. I can't tell you what killed him, because it's not important to what I have to do."

"How can you say it's not important? He's dead. Someone did this, right? I mean, he didn't just have a heart attack and hit his head. . ." I braved another glance down at the body. "No. It looks like he was shot."

"Yeah, it looks that way to me, too. And I don't mean it isn't important, but I have a limited time to move along a soul to his or her destination. I can't stop for chit chat." He took a deep breath and exhaled. "Besides, believe it or not, how a person's physical body dies isn't important to him or her once it's been vacated." As I began to speak, he held up his hand again. "I'm not saying it doesn't matter to you, or even to me, but Al truly doesn't care."

"How do you know? Did you ask him? Was he. . .was his spirit here?"

"His soul was, yes. And no, I didn't ask him. He wouldn't have answered me."

I sniffled and took one more shuddering breath. "Did he know I was here, Lucas? Did Al know I was here?"

Lucas closed his eyes. "Jackie, he—his soul was on a different plane. No, he couldn't see you. He didn't see the restaurant, either, or his body. He only saw the advocates and me."

"The advocates?" I wrinkled my forehead.

"The two men who were here. Listen, I promise I'll tell you everything I know, but we need to leave now. I'm protected from any culpability in a violent death, apparently. Or so I'm told. But I have no idea about you. And the last thing we need is for the police to show up and start asking why you're standing over a body."

"But how? Where are we going?"

Lucas wrapped his arms around me and tucked my head beneath his chin, effectively cutting off my words. Out of instinct, I circled my hands to his back and clutched at his shirt.

"Hang on."

Before I could take another breath, we were back in the

vortex, swirling and swinging and dropping. I screwed shut my eyes and held tight.

Chapter 6

"HERE." LUCAS SET a mug down on the table in front of me, and out of instinct, I picked it up and took a sip. It was tea, some kind of herbal blend, and it tasted like springtime and daffodils. I closed my eyes and breathed in the steam.

"Jackie, I know you have a million questions. The fact that you're not in shock or passed out on the floor—or worse, running screaming down the street, just to get away from me—is a minor miracle. But we're here now. So ask me. Ask me anything."

"What is this?" I lifted the cup.

Lucas's brows drew together. "The tea? That's what you want to know? God, Jackie. . .tonight I told you I think I'm a vampire, something you don't even believe exists, and then I accidentally transport you to a death Reckoning, and the soul in question just happens to be one of your dearest friends. And when I tell you to ask me anything you want, you ask about the tea? It's Springtime in Paris, by the way. One of my students gave it to me for Christmas last year."

I lifted my shoulder in a shrug. "It's good. I like it." I drank some more. "How long? How long have you been—this? Whatever you are?"

He looked over my shoulder, his gaze losing focus. "I think it happened the same night as my. . .the night of my farewell party. I didn't know it, because it was overshadowed by the whole drinking-blood deal, but the guy who delivered that first cooler of blood. . .I knew when he was going to die. It was like this voice in my head whispering how long he had. I thought it was a symptom of whatever other freaky thing was happening to me, but when I met the first advocates, they told me it was part of being a broker."

I nodded as though any of this made sense. "There was a voice whispering in your head?"

Lucas leaned back in his chair. "Yeah. At least, it started out whispering. Then it got louder. And I could see the numbers, too. I just figured the whole thing was part of some weird drug trip. That Veronica had slipped me something, and now I was dealing with the after-effects. The voice in my head seriously spooked me, but it went away when the delivery man left. And then the next person I met, I could hear it again." He met my eyes and then glanced away. "It's the worse part of being a broker. And let me tell you, that's saying something."

I traced the handle of my mug. "So when you met me, you could hear how long I have? When I'm going to die?"

He shook his head. "No, I couldn't. I have no idea why. And at first, I didn't realize it, because I was too busy worrying about other shit going down. Right after I got here, the first night, I got called to my first Reckoning. And yeah, that just about pushed me over the edge of sanity."

"You had no idea at that point? What you were—what you are?"

"Not a clue. According to the advocates, usually there's a process, and a sort of training period. But for some reason, that didn't happen for me. I was sitting here at home, and you had just dropped off the food. And then I started feeling odd. . .it's almost like I'm being pulled by a different kind of gravity. Away from the earth, not toward it. I got dizzy, thought I'd passed out, and when I opened my eyes, I was at a nursing home. And there were two people there talking to me like I should know what I'm doing, but of course, I didn't." He rubbed the back of his neck. "They explained as much as they could."

"What are their names? The advocates?" I thought of the two men I'd met tonight. Neither of them had introduced themselves.

Lucas shrugged. "I don't know. It's a different set each time. There are teams of advocates for both the light and the dark, and I guess there's no set territory for them. They're sent when and where they're needed."

"How does it work, exactly? Can you tell me that? Are you allowed?"

One side of his mouth lifted in a half-smile. "No one's told me any rules, so as far as I know, I can tell you anything I want. And if someone in charge wants to punish me for that—well, that's fucked up, because none of them have told me diddly squat. I'm making my own way here."

"Do you think you could get in trouble? Will someone smite you?"

"I doubt it. The advocates tonight seemed surprised to see you, but they weren't upset. To answer your question, as far as I understand it now, when a person dies, his soul passes to a new plane, where he's met by an advocate from each side. The light and the dark. And I'm the broker: I listen to the arguments, and I determine where the soul goes."

"To heaven or to hell?" I frowned. I was raised Catholic, the product of two families whose lives were deeply entwined with the Church. None of this sounded like what I'd been taught in CCD.

Lucas hesitated. "I'm not sure the same terms apply here.

The advocates describe the destinations as Separation and the Great Beyond. Like I said, I'm still figuring it out, but that's what they say."

"And so what happened to Al tonight? He went to heaven, right?"

"He's in Paradise, yes, which as I understand it, would be the same as your term for heaven."

"You said something about there being no Reckoning because of Grace. What did that mean? Who's Grace? His wife was named Elisabett."

Lucas laughed. "Grace isn't a person in this case, it's a state of being. It means that at some point in his life, Al was redeemed by Grace. Usually, I guess, that means the person was baptized. So there's no need for an accounting. He moved on without it."

"But what if he were a really terrible person who just happened to have gotten dunked at some point? Why should he get to go to heaven then?"

"Jackie, I don't know much about theology. I'm just starting to get the hang of how all this works. But one of the advocates of light told me that being covered by Grace doesn't necessarily mean the soul goes to directly to what you would call heaven. It just means he gets another chance to choose." He stared down at the table for a minute. "At some point, I have to trust that there's a plan, and that someone knows how it all works. Because I can tell you, it ain't me."

I finished my tea and pushed back the cup. It felt as though I'd stumbled into some bizarre universe tonight, and I realized that in order to cope with it, I was segregating everything into manageable chunks. The death broker part was incredible, but I'd lived that. I'd spun through the darkness at Lucas's side, landed at the diner and seen first-hand how it worked. I could handle that. The so-called vampire part. . .that was still murky, something that I wasn't sure about.

And even while my mind was spinning, trying to make sense of anything that had happened since I'd knocked on Lucas's door, my heart was breaking, thinking of Al lying cold and alone on the floor of his restaurant. I wondered if he'd been discovered, if the police were there. Would they be able to figure out who'd killed him? I just couldn't fathom who would want to shoot this man whose only vices had been food and kindness. I thought of his children, all of whom still lived up in New Jersey and New York. They were a close family, and I knew they were going to be devastated.

"Jackie. . .you've had a long night. Why don't you go get some sleep?"

I brought my attention back to Lucas. His hair was mussed, and beneath the sexy-professor glasses, I could see smudges under his eyes. He was exhausted, too. I saw his gaze dart to the fridge next to us, and realization dawned on me.

"Do you need. . .are you thirsty?"

He grimaced. "I wish I could say no, but if I'm telling you the truth, yes, I need to have. . .something. And I really don't want to drink in front of you."

I laughed, a humorless bark. "Yeah, I appreciate that. I like to think I'm open-minded, but I think that just might push me over the edge tonight." I rose and pushed in my chair. "Will you. . .do you have any more, um, Reckonings tonight? Or can you sleep?"

He sighed. "I never know, but so far there haven't been more than one a night or day, and there've been a few days I haven't been called at all. Two tonight is a record. I'm going to drink and then crawl into bed myself."

I tilted my head. "Do you sleep, then?"

"Yeah, I do. Quite a bit, actually." Lucas smiled, and even with everything that had happened in the last few hours, my heart skipped a beat and that part of me that only wanted to be held by him stirred.

"I want to talk to you about that—the vampire part—tomorrow. But I think you're right. I need some rest, and so do you." I stood for a minute, unsure of what to do next. Did I just leave?

Or would he—did he want to kiss me goodnight? Did I want him to do that?

Understanding softened his eyes, and he took one cautious step toward me. "Okay. I'll come over tomorrow, and we'll talk more." He laid one tentative hand on my arm and leaned down to kiss the top of my head. "Sleep well, Jackie."

I swallowed hard. "You, too."

I slipped out into the cool damp of midnight and walked over the wet the grass. The dark was still and silent, and normally, I might have been a little spooked. A little wary of what lurked in the shadows. But tonight, after everything I'd seen and heard, I was more concerned about what lived next door than what watched me in the night.

I'd expected to have trouble shutting down my mind that night, but once I'd locked my door behind me after taking Makani out for a quick visit to the bushes, I collapsed into bed on top of the covers. I didn't stir until pounding on my front door woke me.

Makani rolled over and whined a little. I looked at him through bleary eyes. "Just a minute, baby. Let me see who Mommy has to kill for waking us up this morning."

I was still dressed in my shorts and T-shirt from the night before, so I just ran a hand over my messy hair and dragged myself to the front door. I'd expected it to be Lucas—with coffee and something sweet if he knew anything about women—but instead, I saw Mrs. Mac. She was holding a wadded-up tissue, and her eyes were red.

Suddenly the night before came tumbling on top of me. *Al.* Mrs. Mac must've heard. I unlocked the door and took a deep breath.

"Oh, Jackie, are you just getting up?" She frowned up at me. "Did I wake you? Sorry, dear." She stepped inside, and I stood back automatically, swallowing over the lump in my throat.

"Mrs. Mac, what's wrong?" My voice was rough from sleep, and I rubbed at my eyes. "Are you all right?"

"No, sweetie, I'm not. I'm sorry to do this, to wake you up with bad news, but it'd better for you to hear it from me." She sank onto one of my kitchen chairs and clutched at my hand. "Jackie, it's Al. He's. . .he's passed."

I hadn't thought I would cry. After all, this wasn't news to me. I'd seen him last night. But hearing the words come out of Mrs. Mac's mouth somehow made his death solid and irreversible. I sat down across from her and buried my face in my hands as sobs shook me.

"I know." She was weeping again, too. "And Jackie, that's not the worst of it, I'm afraid. He didn't just. . .they found him in the diner. He'd been shot."

I didn't raise my head, afraid she'd see the knowledge in my eyes. "My God, who would do that?"

"They don't know, honey. The police are looking into it, but it doesn't look like robbery, from what I heard. But what else? Who would want to hurt that sweet harmless man?" She laid her head down on the table, and her shoulders shook.

I stood to wrap my arms around her. "I know, Mrs. Mac. Please, don't get yourself too upset. Remember your blood pressure." A thought struck me as I patted her heaving back. Lucas. . .he'd known Al was going to die. And did he know about Mrs. Mac, too? How much longer I had with her? Anger welled in me. How could he not have told me?

For half an hour, we sat together, crying and trying to make sense of the senseless. Mrs. Mac told me that Al's family had been notified overnight, and apparently they were expected to arrive later in the day. I'd met them all at one time or another over the past four years, but I dreaded seeing them again, under these circumstances. Part of me wished I could tell them what

I knew: that their beloved father had moved on to heaven, that the manner of his death hadn't mattered to him at all once it was done. But of course, I could never say that.

The rest of the day was a blur of grief and tears. Neighbors were in and out of the house, each visitor bringing a fresh wave of news and speculation. Given how close the diner was to our development, there was also an element of fear, as everyone worried about our safety in our homes.

"It's not like the old days, when you could leave your doors unlocked all the time." Mr. Rivers wagged his head. "Why, when I was a boy, we didn't even have a key to our front door. We just walked in and out, never giving it a thought. Sad thing when a man isn't safe even his own business."

"I barely sleep now as it is." Mrs. Nelson clutched her hands in her lap. "Since Len died, every noise, every creak wakes me up. Now I'll be worried even more. I wonder if I should get another dog."

I got up to put on a new pot of coffee. I wasn't sure why my house had become the central gathering place for those of us in shock at Al's passing, but it had. The only person on the block I hadn't seen today was Lucas. No one else found that odd, since he hadn't known Al well at all. Still, I kept looking through the window, half-hoping and half-dreading to see him heading my way.

A few of the ladies brought over the traditional casseroles, and just as we were sitting down to eat, Al's youngest daughter Dena arrived. Of all his children, she was the one I knew the best, despite the fact that she was twenty years older than me, and it didn't surprise me that she'd come by. As everyone fussed over her, I steeled myself against a brand new onslaught of weeping.

Dena told us about the plans that had been put into motion for a memorial service down here in Florida.

"We want to do something to honor the last years of his life, with all of you." She smiled at us through wet eyes. "Daddy wanted to be cremated, so once the—the police release him to us, we'll do that and then take him home to do a funeral Mass there. He'll be put to rest next to Mama."

"It's what he wanted." All the heads around the table nodded. Down here, death was not an abstract idea, something that could be pushed off and thought about later. It was part of our reality, an inevitability that everyone in my neighborhood had already planned out.

"Dena, sweetie, I'm sorry to ask you, but do the police have any more information on what happened? Who would do this terrible thing?" Mrs. Nelson leaned forward.

Dena shook her head. "Not that they're telling us. The last person to see him was Mary. She was working the dinner shift, and she said he asked her to close up for him, which wasn't unusual if he had plans or was just tired. She said he seemed a little distracted, but the detective said that could just be her perception in retrospect." Dena met my eyes. "Jackie, did you see him yesterday?"

I swallowed. "No, I. . .I didn't talk to him. Not since earlier in the week. I stopped in for breakfast and gave him the names of some of the photographers I'd found for the cookbook. He was in the middle of the rush, so we really didn't speak long. I told him I'd stop by later." I bit back another sob. "We were supposed to begin cooking for the book this weekend. He was so excited."

"He was. I just wish I knew why he went back to the restaurant last night." Dena wiped her eyes. "There wasn't any sign of breaking and entering, so the police are pretty sure he let in whoever it was. Someone he knew."

"How anyone who knew that man could hurt him. . ." Mrs. Mac smoothed her napkin with trembling fingers. "I just don't see it."

"None of us can." Dena tried to smile. "Daddy was the best man I ever knew. He'd never hurt anything or anyone. I just can't understand it."

92

And so the loop began again, with everyone voicing questions that none of us had any hope of answering. My head began to pound as the past twenty-four hours started to catch up with me.

When Dena left a little while later, the rest of my company began to trickle out as well. I finally closed the door behind the last one at just after nine. I collapsed onto the sofa, and Makani licked my hand, whether in hopes of a second dinner or in an effort to comfort me, I wasn't sure.

After a few minutes of wallowing, I sat up and looked out the window. One light shone at the house next door. I poured a glass of shiraz and dragged myself up and out to the porch, taking up my usual spot on the rocking chair. Makani trotted out with me and sat at my feet, sniffing the air with interest.

"What do you smell, baby? Is there a possum out there?"

"No, just your friendly neighborhood bloodsucker." The voice that came out of the darkness was deep and slightly ironic.

I startled, bringing both feet down flat onto the porch. "My God, Lucas! You scared the hell out of me."

"Sorry." He stepped into the dim light and sat down on the step. "I saw you come out, and I thought it was probably safe to come over."

"You could've come earlier." I curled my knees up to my chest and hugged them. "Everyone was here."

"Which was why I didn't." He ran his hand through his hair. "I couldn't deal with all those people. The noise of the numbers would've been deafening. And it wouldn't have felt right for me to be with all of you who knew Al so well. I would've felt like an intruder."

I'd thought I was all cried out, but tears filled my eyes anyway. "You could've been here for me. It was a hard day. Everyone was talking about Al, and I kept seeing him, bleeding on the floor. I had to pretend to be like the rest of them."

Lucas closed his eyes. "I'm sorry, Jackie. Sorry I couldn't be here for you today, and sorry about you seeing Al last night.

Of all the times for you to be with me when I was called. . .I don't know why it had to be that one."

I watched the way his hands moved his forehead, and despite everything, the day, the grief and the pain, I still felt a surge of want. In fact, if anything, the urge was stronger. I wanted to slither off the chair and crawl over to him, lay him flat on the wooden floor and cover his body with mine. A thread of desire ran down my middle to between my legs, and I licked my lips.

"Jackie?"

Lucas spoke again, questioning and hesitant, and I yanked my attention back to him. Rather, to what he was saying.

"Yeah. Sorry. . .distracted. Um, that's not a picture I wanted in my mind. Everyone else gets to remember Al like he was: alive and funny and loving."

"Pretty soon, that's what you'll remember, too." Lucas slid closer to me and touched my foot where it rested on the edge of the rocking chair. "The good memories will replace that last bad image."

"I still want to know what happened. I can't believe you get to judge souls, but you can't find out how they died. That seems like a bad plan."

Lucas rubbed the top of my toes, making me shiver. "I don't really judge the souls. I just use the guidelines I was given to tell them where they have to go."

"I meant to ask you. What was up with your eyes, doing that weird glowing thing last night?"

"What weird glowing thing?" Lucas frowned at me.

"Right before you said the thing about Al being covered by Grace. Your eyes. . .they kind of went golden. Like whisky-colored, and they glowed."

"Really?" Apparently this was news to Lucas. "Huh. I didn't know that. But then, the only people around during a Reckoning are the advocates, and it probably wouldn't seem out of the ordinary for them." He moved his hand up to my ankle, tracing small circles on my skin. "You know, my eyes used to be blue."

I shifted a little to give him better access. My heartbeat picked up speed the more he touched me. "Oh, yeah?"

"The morning after. . .Veronica, when I woke up, my eyes were brown. I didn't realize it right away. I thought it was a vampire thing, but maybe it was more of a broker thing."

I sighed as his fingers skimmed up the back of my calf. "Hmmm. You seem pretty hung up on the idea of being a vampire. How do you know that drinking blood isn't part of being a broker?"

"I figured it was, until I mentioned something to the advocates that first night. I started babbling about the change and the blood, and the one from light looked at me like I was speaking a foreign language. I got them to tell me what I could expect as a broker, and drinking blood was not part of it."

"Oh." I tried to keep the disappointment out of my voice.

"I know." Lucas sounded grim, but his fingers were gentle as they curved around my leg. "It would be so much easier if I were one thing or another, right? I could deal with being a death broker, I think. I mean, now that I am. I wouldn't ask for the job, of course. It wasn't on my list of future careers when I graduated from high school a million years ago. If that's what I'm destined to do, I'd accept it. But tossing the vampire on top of it just sucks."

We were silent for a minute. I bit my lip, but I couldn't hold in the burst of laughter. My head fell back against the chair, and I wrapped my arms around my middle as my whole body shook. Lucas held tight to my leg and leaned his forehead onto it, his back moving up and down, too.

"Vampire—sucks." I gasped the words. "You did not just say that."

"It wasn't that funny, Jackie." But he was still chuckling, his breath hot on the bare skin of my leg. I let my head loll to the side and lifted one hand to touch his head. The hair beneath my palm was soft, nearly baby-fine, and I let it sift through my fingers. Lucas closed his eyes again and brought his face closer to my calf. He inhaled deeply. I would've thought he was sniffing my skin, checking out my body lotion, if he were anyone else. If I hadn't know what he was.

And in that moment, it flooded over me, the knowing of it. Last night, I would've denied it was possible. I would've sworn such a thing couldn't exist. But tonight, my belief trumped logic and rationality. I didn't know any details, I had no idea how such things could be possible, but there was no doubt in my mind that Lucas was something extraordinary.

I didn't care. The thrumming in my blood could only find one answer, and it lay in the man who now sat at my feet. His eyes met mine, and all humor fled. His pupils were dilated as he stared up at me. He shifted his head just enough that his mouth touched me. I felt the tip of his tongue against my skin, tasting, tracing, teasing.

Lucas didn't move further. There was a question in his eyes, and I knew he was waiting for my permission. All I had to do was pull away the slightest bit, and he would stop. He might've been a death broker, he might've been a vampire—or half a vamp, whatever that meant—but my sexy professor was above all a gentleman. He wouldn't push me into anything I wasn't absolutely sure I wanted.

I wasn't certain of anything at this point except that I did want this. I wanted him. If I'd taken time to consider, to weigh my options, I might've made a smarter choice. But I was tired, so damned sick and tired of being careful and cautious. I was done. I was ready.

So instead of moving back, I ran my hand down the side of his cheek to the line of his jaw. I raked the light stubble on his chin with the tip of my nail. His skin was warm, nothing like the hard, cold flesh described in vampire lore. Fleetingly I wondered if this were because the stories were wrong or if that just wasn't part of Lucas's particular strain.

My finger reached the side of his mouth, and Lucas turned his head to suck on it. I caught my breath as his tongue stroked the pad. He rose up on his knees, his arms sliding around my waist. I dropped my hand from his lips and let my feet lower to the ground. Lucas paused, his expression inscrutable.

"Jackie. . ." He spoke barely above a whisper, and I leaned forward to hear him. "Do you want to go inside?"

A slow smile curved my lips. "Oh, yeah. I really do.'

He nodded, but his face stayed serious. "I don't know what's going to happen. I don't know if I might. . .hurt you. I don't think I could, but you have to be aware of it up front. I can leave now, and I wouldn't blame you for asking me to do that."

I cupped my palm around his cheek. "I don't believe you could. But I promise, if I feel at all like I'm in danger—that you're out of control—I'll stop you."

He leaned in again until his mouth was at my ear. "Out of control doesn't have to be a bad thing."

Chapter 7

MAKANI FOLLOWED US into the house, and I scooped him up, heading to the back door. Lucas looked at me with one raised brow.

"I need to take him out in the back one more time and then crate him. It's his bedtime, first of all, and second. . .there's never been a man in the house who. . ." I tried to figure out how to say what I meant without being presumptuous about what was going to happen. "Well, other than my family or neighbors. I'm not sure how he'll react."

"Okay." Lucas glanced around my living room. "I'll just sit down here while you take care of him. Unless you want me to take him out for you first? I don't mind."

I smiled. "That would be great. Just outside the back door, and he usually performs pretty fast at night. I'll get his treat and water ready." I set the pup on the floor and nudged him with my foot. "Go on, Makani. Go with Lucas."

He looked up at me and then over at the man in question.

"C'mon, buddy. Let's go do your thing so you can get your

treat." Lucas spoke the magic words, and Makani trotted after him through the kitchen to the back door. I refreshed the water dish and dug out his favor brand of Uncle Jimmie treats from under the sink. When the two males in my life came in a few minutes later, both seemed inordinately satisfied with themselves.

"He did everything he was suppose to." Lucas grinned. "He earned his treat."

"Wonderful." I held up the little square of doggy goodness. "What'll you do for an Uncle Jimmie treat?"

Makani went through his nightly ritual of dance like a diva, high-five and speak before he dropped to his back to squirm. I laid down the treat on the floor and counted to three before I nodded. "Okay, go."

His little body gyrated over and gobbled up his reward. Lucas laughed.

"All of that for one little treat? You've got high expectations, lady."

I smiled up at him from under my lashes. "You have no idea. But let me tell you. . .when I give you a treat, you'll appreciate it all the more for the effort it takes."

The temperature in the room seemed to rise about ten degrees as all humor fled from Lucas's face, replaced by a need that was deadly serious. His eyes darkened again, and I watched in fascination as his tongue shot out to lick his lips. When he spoke, his tone was even but intense.

"Put the pup to bed, Jackie."

I was tempted to tease a bit more, but something in his face told me play time was over. I picked up Makani and his water bowl and headed for the bedroom. I half expected Lucas to follow us, but he stayed in the living room while I settled the dog for the night.

I hooked the crate, and the puppy turned in his typical three circles before he lay down with a very human sigh. I whispered good night to him and turned to go out, stopping in mid-stride when I caught sight of myself in the mirror.

The only light in the bedroom was coming in from the hallway, but I could see enough. My eyes were still puffy from a day of crying, and my skin was devoid of makeup. I'd showered quickly during a break in visitors, but I hadn't taken the time to dry my hair, so it hung in waves down my back. From where I stood, I looked every minute of my way-past-thirty years.

The thought of how Lucas must see me nearly sent me diving under the covers of my bed to hide from him. An image of Cathryn flashed across my mind, and I shuddered. Her smooth alabaster skin, perfect hair and tight little body made me feel old, sloppy and clumsy. And Lucas had admitted they'd been together this past summer. If he compared me to her, how in the world could I not come out lacking?

I closed my eyes and drew in a long cleansing breath, like we did in yoga. And then I lectured myself. *You are who Lucas wants right now. The look in his eyes. . .there's no mistaking what it means. Even if it's just the scent of your blood that drives him crazy. . .at least something about you does. Go out there and be the strong, confident woman I know you are.*

I grinned, knowing that last line had downloaded in my brain directly from Leesa. One more deep breath and I turned to go out, closing the door behind me.

Lucas was sprawled on the couch, the remote in his hand as he flipped through channels. The TV was on mute, and I shook my head as I sat down on the other end of the sofa.

"What?" He spared me a sideways look before the images on the screen stole his attention back.

"Men. Put you in a room with a television set, and you go on the hunt. You know there's a guide on there, right? You can just see what's on and click the show you want to watch. No more surfing needed."

He grinned, bringing out the dimple to tease me. Yup, I was a goner. "But that's the fun in it. The surfing. There's nothing on here I want to watch, I was just killing time until you came out."

"And here I am." I swung my feet up to rest on the cushion

er-smaller circles around my hardening nipple, until he finally took it between his thumb and forefinger. I arched my back as he pinched it, sucking harder at my belly button ring at the same time. The pull of need stretched down between my legs, wanting him there now. I struggled, unsure of how to get him to move.

"Jackie." Lucas rested his cheek on my stomach. "I need to. . ." He swallowed, and I watched his Adam's apple work up and down in his throat. "I haven't been with anyone since I was. . .changed. I don't know what's happening, except that for the first time, I want someone's blood. Yours. The craving is insane. I want to make love to you, I want to be inside you, but I can almost taste you at the same time. It's like the desires are linked."

I wasn't sure how to respond to that. Lucas ran his tongue over my skin again and then pushed himself up so that he leaned over me, looking down into my eyes.

"Do you trust me, Jackie?"

I wanted to say yes, and partly, it was the truth. Lucas hadn't lied to me, as far as I knew. He'd tried to keep himself away from me, tried to avoid getting tangled up. I didn't have any doubts about the sexy professor part. But the gleam in his eye was that of a hunter, someone who would not be denied. While I couldn't say I didn't have reservations, I had to admit that it was that part of him that made me want to ignore every warning bell in my head and open my body to him.

Lucas was waiting for my answer. I met his eyes and whispered the word.

"Yes."

He reared back and gripped the hem of my shirt. "Then take this off. And your shorts, too. I want to see all of you."

As I scooted back to strip off my clothes, he crossed his arms over his front and pulled off his own T-shirt, then sat back on his haunches to look at me. I'd tossed my bra to the side with my shirt and shorts, and I only wore the cotton bikinis I'd put on this afternoon.

Lucas ran his eyes down my body and made a sound low in

his throat. "I promise I won't hurt you. But if you feel uncomfortable or freaked out, tell me and I'll stop. Okay?"

I nodded and reached to touch him. "Were you always this built, or is this part of the vampire thing?"

He chuckled, taking my hand and bringing it to his lips. "I'm glad you think I am, but no, that wasn't one of the changes. As far as I've seen, the only real symptoms I have are the blood drinking and the garlic aversion."

I let my palm roam over his chest. "What about sunlight? And immortality?"

"Direct, bright sunlight gives me a headache, but it doesn't burn me or make me sparkle." Lucas dipped his head to kiss me, slow and sensuous. "Living forever. . .I have no idea. I haven't tested that theory yet." He lowered his hand to my breast, cupping it and moving his thumb around the pink tip, which hardened at his touch. "But I have a feeling tonight may be night."

I pushed up on my elbows. "What do you mean?"

A slow smile spread over his face. "Because right now I'm feeling like I might die if I can't touch you." He brought his mouth down to take the place of his hand on my breast, and I fell back onto the couch. I threaded my fingers through the hair on the back of his head, murmuring encouragement as he sucked my nipple into his mouth.

"Lucas. . ." I ran my hands restlessly up and down his back as he moved his lips from one boob to the other. Just when I thought I might be the one to spontaneously combust, he began kissing down the center of my torso, pausing at the navel ring again to let his mouth play with it. The tug of the ring sent a new thrill of desire down between my legs, and as if he could sense that, Lucas covered me with his hand, rubbing over my underwear. I raised my hips to meet both hand and mouth better, and he slid two fingers beneath the cotton to touch me.

I was slick with want. Lucas mumbled some words against my stomach, but I was too busy coming apart at the feeling of the gentle friction as he explored me, pushing against the tiny bundle of nerves and then plunging his fingers into me. Just on the edge of my climax, he stopped, pulling his hand away.

"Lucas." I spoke this time through gritted teeth. "If you stop what you're doing, we're going to find out whether or not you can live forever right here and now, because I swear I'll kill you."

He laughed. "Patience, sweetheart. I just wanted to get all barriers out of my way." He hooked his thumbs around the edge of my panties and dragged them down my legs and over my feet, dropping them onto the growing pile of clothes. He settled lower between my legs, pushing them a little further apart.

"You see? Good things come to those who wait." His breath teased against my sensitive flesh.

I writhed, hissing. "'Come' better be the operative word in that sentence, buddy."

He didn't answer. Instead, he licked up the inside of my thigh, pausing at the ridge of muscle just below the juncture of my legs.

"This. . ." He growled the word and bit me softly. "This right here makes me insane."

Before I could respond, his mouth finally covered my swollen sex, lips and tongue stroking and sucking. Every nerve in my body was on fire, and everything in the world centered right there. Pleasure pulsed ever faster, building to a crescendo.

I gripped his head against me, lifting my hips to grind against his mouth. As I tensed, on the edge of coming, I felt a sharp stinging at the spot he had bitten moments before, and then his fingers were on my pussy, moving faster and faster, and his mouth had lowered to the inside of my leg. The orgasm that gripped me was the most intense, mind-blowing sensation I'd ever felt, and I screamed his name over and over as my hips worked up and down.

Lucas slowed his fingers, stroking me down, and his tongue circled the place on my leg he'd sucked. My breath began to slow to a normal rate, but I wasn't sure I'd ever move again. My bones had melted right here on this couch, and I was perfectly okay with that.

I barely registered his kisses up my stomach and between my breasts until his head was even with mine again. He wore an expression that was a mix of bliss and desire, and I remembered the bite and the stinging.

"What did you do? On my leg, I mean." I realized I sounded less than grateful—after all, the man had just given me what was undoubtedly the best orgasm of my life—but I had to admit I was more than a little unsettled at the idea of him drinking my blood.

Lucas glanced down my body, and I picked up the glimmer of guilt in his eyes. "It was like I had to do it. I had to. . .taste you. I didn't actually bite you deep, though. Just enough to break the skin. It's not even bleeding anymore." He paused, searching my face for some sign of how freaked out I really was.

"I. . ." I bit my lip. "Lucas, you've got to understand. I'm not the most experienced woman when it comes to sex, and what I do know has been pretty vanilla. Basic. So, yeah, that's a little bit on the wild side for me. And I guess I have to admit that I'm still not sure what to think of this whole vampire idea. What if it's something else completely?"

He squeezed himself into the space between my body and the back of the sofa, sighing. "Jackie, I didn't taste your blood because I felt it was something a vampire would do. It was. . .a compulsion. In the heat of the moment, I couldn't *not* do it." He trailed a finger between my breasts. "Any more than if I were inside you, I wouldn't be able to *not* come. It was like a pounding in my head." He captured one of my nipples between his fingers, and I drew in a shuddering breath. I felt him against my hip, his erection hard through his shorts.

I slid my hand between our bodies and wrapped my fingers around his length. He moaned and shifted to give me better access.

"So you're saying if I were. . .in the same position, and I decided to make you bleed and taste it, you'd be okay with that?"

Lucas raised himself on his arms and looked down at me. The dangerous glint was back, and so was the dimple. Damn, I didn't stand a chance.

"If you were in the same position, lying between my legs with my cock in your mouth. . .you could do whatever the hell you wanted. Other than bite it off, of course." One side of his mouth lifted. "But do you really want to drink my blood?"

"God, no. That's disgusting." I made a face, and Lucas collapsed back onto the couch, careful to avoid dropping his weight onto me as he laughed.

"Does it disgust you that I did it?" He was keeping his voice neutral, but I could tell he was concerned, no matter how much I amused him.

"No. Not disgust." I hesitated, thinking. "Concern, I guess. And. . ." This was harder to explain. "I think part of that is wondering if you only want me for my blood. If the rest of me doesn't matter to you."

Lucas gathered me against him. "That's absolutely not true. If you told me that I couldn't taste you again, I'd still desire the hell out of your body. I'd still want to touch you, make you come. . ." He pressed against me, reminding me not-so-subtly that his arousal was still right there by my hand. "Let you touch me. However you wanted to. Whenever you wanted to."

I rolled my eyes. "You're such a man. You might be a death broker and a sort-of vampire, but deep down, you just want me to get you off."

Lucas kissed my ear lobe. "That may be the best compliment I've ever had. Yes, please."

"Hmmm." I pushed myself up so that now I leaned over his body. And what a body it was. His firm chest was rivaled only by the tight abs, all lightly dusted with brown hair that formed a trail leading down to the button on his shorts. I gave him a saucy smile as I flicked it open. "Oh my! Look what just happened there."

"Yeah, look at that. What're you going to do about it?" He put his hands behind his head to watch me.

"I guess I'll have to do. . .this." I found the tab of the zipper and tugged it down, letting my fingers caress the hard ridge beneath. Lucas groaned, and I grinned. "And then I think I should probably do this next." I wriggled my fingers into the opening of his shorts and through the placket of his boxers, covering him with my palm, skin to skin at last.

"God, Jackie, that's—no." He ground out the last word, and I looked back at him, puzzled. He didn't want me to touch him? What was up with that?

"For the love of anything and everything holy—why now? Shit, damn, hell, fuck." Lucas struggled to sit up. "Jackie, I'm sorry. I'm about to be called. Better move away from me. I'm pretty sure you'll only be transported with me if we're touching. I'm so sorry about this."

I slid to the floor and grabbed for our pile of clothes. "No reason for you to be sorry. I feel amazing. You're the one who didn't—uh, get to finish." I found his shirt and turned it right side out. "Here you go."

But when I turned, he was gone. I sat there on the floor for a few minutes, staring at the spot on the couch where he'd been and still holding his shirt. I'd heard of men leaving fast after sex, but this had to be new record.

I sighed, gathered up our clothes and went to bed. By myself.

Chapter 8

WHEN I OPENED my eyes the next morning, I was immediately aware that I wasn't alone. And it wasn't the pup in bed with me this time. Strong arms circled my waist, snugging my back against a hard body.

Hard was definitely the key word here.

I'd half-expected Lucas to come back to my house after his Reckoning call. After all, as he'd pointed out, he *was* a man, and last night he'd been a man interrupted in the middle of sex. No one would fault him for wanting to pick up where we'd left off. Least of all me.

But he hadn't returned by the time I'd climbed into bed, and the combination of the day of mourning and the night of passion knocked me into a deep sleep faster than I'd expected. As I looked down at his hands, relaxed in sleep and lying just beyond my boobs on the mattress, I wondered how long he'd been here with me. And why he hadn't woken me up when he'd come in.

"I can feel you thinking, Jackie. It's too early."

I shifted within his embrace. "You cannot feel me thinking."

I paused, suddenly doubtful. "Can you?"

He shook once with a short laugh. "No, but I could feel you start to tense, and your breathing changed. You're lying there wondering when I got here, what happened last night, and what comes next."

I turned so that I could face him, and his arms slid around to hold me tighter as I spoke. "Smart-ass. You got one of out three right. I did wonder when you came in and why you didn't wake up."

His lips curved, but his eyes stayed closed. "I got in about three. Apparently—and I didn't know this until last night—I get transported back to wherever I was when the call came in, so I ended up back in your living room, not at my house as I'd thought. I considered grabbing my shirt and walking home, and then I came in to check on you, and I decided to take off the rest of my clothes and climb into bed with you, instead."

Warmth swelled within me. "I'm glad you did. It was nice waking up with you."

"And the reason I didn't wake you up to finish what we started? You looked too peaceful, and I remembered what you said about me just being here for you while you're grieving. So that's what I wanted to do."

I leaned up to kiss him. "Thank you." Settling back down under the covers, I tried to drift off to sleep again, but my mind wouldn't quiet. I thought of Al, and with a pang I wondered if the police were any closer to finding the killer. The memorial service was tomorrow, and while I knew it wouldn't comfort his children to know the truth, it might bring us all some sense of justice.

Thinking of Al and all of my older friends brought to mind something that had been lurking for the last day. "Lucas. . .you knew when Al was going to die, didn't you? When you met him that day. . .you heard it. And you didn't tell me."

He stroked one hand down my back. "Yes, I did. I'm sorry. At the time I met him, you didn't know about me yet. What was

I supposed to say? 'Hey, don't get attached. He's not going to be around much longer.'"

"No. But. . ." I wanted there to be a way he could've warned me, but I knew Lucas was right. Still. . . "So you know when Mrs. Mac and Mr. Rivers and everyone else is going to die, too?"

He sighed. "Did I hear the time when I met them? Yes. Do I remember? No. I hear that so much, Jackie. I push it out of my mind. If I'd realized when I met her that Mrs. Mac was important to you and that you were going to be important to me, I probably would've paid more attention. But I didn't. And I wouldn't tell you even if I did, because it would make you crazy. Why should you have to suffer when you could be blissfully ignorant like the rest of the world?"

I rested my forehead on Lucas's shoulder. "I could be prepared. I'd know to be ready when the last times came."

"Jackie, that's not how life works. Isn't it better that you appreciate her all the time rather than worrying as it gets closer?"

I wasn't ready to concede that, but I couldn't come up with any decent argument either. I settled for making a non-committal hum. Lucas brushed back the hair from my face and kissed my forehead. "Are you hungry? I make a mean omelet."

"You're going to cook for me? Really? And right now? Don't you want. . .you know." I managed to sneak my hand between us, where there was no doubt Lucas was interested in something other than food.

"Of course I do, but I think you should eat. Plus, you're sad again. I don't want to force the issue when you're dealing with so much."

I rolled to my back. "I started to feel guilty after you left last night. I loved Al so much. What does it say about me that I ended up naked with my next door neighbor the night he died?"

Lucas leaned over me and kissed my lips, quickly but firmly. "It says that you honored your friend by embracing life. Appreciating the benefits of a mind-blowing orgasm doesn't make you a bad person."

"Mind-blowing, huh?" I smirked. "Someone's a little cocky."

"Please don't use the word 'little' and 'cock' in the same sentence when I'm naked in bed with you, okay? You'll give a guy a complex. And what you said before? I'd like to think that I'm more than just your next-door neighbor by now."

I pulled him down for another kiss. "I guess you do qualify for a better title. And as far as I can feel. . ." I took him in my hand. "The word little doesn't apply."

"Keep it up and I'll forget I'm trying to be supportive." Lucas rolled over and planted his feet on the floor. "Why don't you see to the pup while I start the eggs?"

"Okay." But I lay still for a few minutes and enjoyed the view as a very fine, very naked Lucas walked across the room to put on his shorts.

"What does his name mean?"

I glanced across the table at Lucas as he forked some eggs onto his wheat toast.

"I'm sorry?"

"The dog. What does Makani mean?"

"Oh." I grinned. "It means 'the wind' in Hawaiian. I spent a lot of time looking for the right name for him, and I thought that was cool. Of course, he doesn't usually run like the wind, unless he's racing into my new neighbor's yard on moving day."

Lucas reached down to knuckle the pup's fluffy head. "He was just welcoming me to the neighborhood, weren't you, boy?" He leaned back in his chair, wiping his hands with the napkin. "So what's on your agenda for today?"

I wasn't used to anyone asking me that question. I cast my

eyes upward. "I'll probably work on next week's column and call Al's daughter Dena to see if they need anything for tomorrow." I dragged a bit of omelet around the plate with my fork. "How about you?"

"I was thinking I might actually write today." He grinned. "You might remember I moved down here to do that. I've been a little distracted, what with the death brokering, the blood drinking and the sexy neighbor."

Pleasure put a smile on my face. "Sexy, really? Are you sure you don't mean nosy and clumsy? The one who falls into your bushes and on top of you?"

Lucas reached across the table to snag my hand and brought my fingertips to his lips. "The day you fell into my bush, I got my first look at your killer ass. And when you fell on me, I totally felt you up. Didn't you realize that?"

I shook my head. "Thanks for trying to make me feel better."

"Seriously, Jackie." He wouldn't let go even when I tried to pull back my hand. "I didn't want you to know what I am. I tried to hide it from you, keep my distance. But because you wouldn't let me do that, I ended up having someone I can share this craziness with. And I can't tell you what a relief that is."

I squeezed his hand, unable to speak. The moment was broken when we both heard a buzzing coming from Lucas's pocket. He leaned back to retrieve his phone and glanced at the screen.

"It's Cathryn. Do you mind if I take it?"

A surge of jealousy welled up in me, but I tamped it down and forced a smile. "Of course not." I stood and carried our dishes to the sink. Lucas stepped out the back door. I could hear his voice, but I couldn't quite make out the words.

I rinsed our plates and loaded the dishwasher. Lucas was still on the phone, so I went into my bedroom and took a shower, hoping he might join me. But no matter how many times I washed, rinsed and repeated, he didn't come in. I dried my hair, dressed and went back to the living room to find him sitting on the sofa with Makani in his lap. Lucas's head was leaned against the back of the couch, eyes closed, with one of his hands buried in the pup's fur.

I tried to walk quietly, but he heard me, his eyes popping open as soon as I came into the room.

"Sorry. Long night catching up with me."

I perched on the edge of the couch next to him, brushing back a lock of hair from his forehead. "Do you want to go lie down in my room? Get a real nap?"

He shook his head. "Thanks, but I think I'll go home and grab a shower." He glanced at me. "Cathryn's coming down to let me know what she's found out. About me. My situation."

I swallowed back that insecurity and managed a smile. "Oh, good. Well, I'm going to work here. I might go over and see Mrs. Mac. She was pretty upset yesterday, and I want to make sure she's okay."

"Hey." Lucas reached for my hand and threaded his fingers through mine. "I was hoping maybe you'd come over to hear what Cathryn has to say. Saves me from having to repeat it to you."

He wanted me to be there. A little of thrill of gladness replaced the ugly green jealousy monster. "Sure, I can do that. Why don't you just call me when you're ready?"

"Sounds good." He leaned to drop a quick kiss on my lips and stood up with one more ruffle of Makani's fur. "By the way, I plan to take you up on your offer from this morning."

I played dumb. "What offer was that?"

He bent over me, his face close to mine. "You know the one. It has to do with you and me being naked together again. And more mind-blowing orgasms for both of us." He straightened up again. "I just figured we needed to get through the next few days before we can relax and enjoy ourselves. I'll see you in a bit."

I listened to the door close behind him and then watched him half-jog across the side yard to his own back door. When I knew he was safely inside, I picked up my cell and pushed one

114

button.

"Hey, Jacks, what's up?" Leesa's voice was distracted; I knew she was at the office. It was mid-morning on a Tuesday, after all.

"You busy?"

She laughed. "Busy is the way of life. But I have a second or two for my bestest ever. Everything all right?"

I lay back on the couch, thinking that twenty years earlier, I'd have been twirling the phone cord on my finger while having this conversation with Leesa. "Yeah, but if you're too busy to hear how I got naked with the neighbor, that's okay. It'll keep until later."

"Jackie!" Her shriek had to have shaken up the rest of her office. "You did not!"

"I did so."

"Hold on." I heard muffled words, and then she came back. "Okay, I'm alone now. And I want every gory detail. But first, is he Spiderman? Did you find out his deal?"

This was going to be tricky, I knew. I had to skirt around what had happened to Lucas, what he was, and the horrifying discovery of Al's body in order to tell Leesa what she really wanted to hear.

"No superhero, but he really is super, if you know what I mean."

She squealed in true best friend fashion. "All right, start at the beginning and tell me everything."

I'd just ended our chat when I spied the blue Thunderbird pulling up outside. I sat still, watching Cathryn get out and walk up Lucas's front walk. Today she was in black gabardine pants and a blue silk shell that I thought probably came close to matching her eyes. She glanced over at my house just before climbing onto the porch.

Once she'd disappeared through the front door, I forced myself to get up and open my laptop. I began organizing the photos I'd taken earlier in the week, selecting which ones I'd send with my column. I attached them to the email along with my article and sent it all off to my editor. I checked my phone to make sure I hadn't missed anything from Lucas. Nothing.

The strong, confident me said I was worrying for nothing. The insecure me warned that Cathryn had changed her mind about Lucas and had lured him into taking her to bed, where he was even now comparing her supple young body with my older one.

Before I could venture too far down the road to crazy town, my phone buzzed with a text. It was from Lucas, and it read: *Are you coming?*

I smiled. *Be right there.*

Lucas was at the door when I came over, opening it before I could ring the bell. He took my hand and pulled me inside, kissing me lightly as he drew me closer to him. I had the sense he was making a point, but I wasn't going to complain.

Cathryn sat on the couch, her face expressionless. Her lips twitched a little, the only indication that she might not have been pleased to see me.

"Jackie." She nodded.

"Sorry we took so long. I wanted to explain to Cathryn that you know everything and that it was okay to talk in front of you."

I glanced at her set face. "I get the feeling maybe Cathryn doesn't agree with you."

Her eyes darted from Lucas to me. "Jackie, it's not that I don't think you're trustworthy, and certainly Lucas is more than capable of choosing with whom he wishes to share his own secrets. But my own business relies heavily on discretion, and he didn't consult me before he exposed me."

"Cathryn, for God's sake. I didn't show Jackie a sex tape with you in it. But in the context of our discussion, I mentioned a very small piece of your job."

"Without checking with me first." She flickered a glance to him, one that I was pretty would have slain a lesser man. Lucas just rolled his eyes.

I wonder if she's really upset about him telling me about her work or because we're together. If we are together. Well, as together as we are. I tried to keep my face as blank as Cathryn's.

"Fine, Cat. Be mad at me. Whatever. But it's done now. Would you like her to sign something in blood?"

"Given what we've been discussing, it would be appropriate. But no, I'm willing to take her word that she has not said anything and will not in the future." Cathryn turned to look at me, one eyebrow raised.

"Of course I haven't and I won't. I promise." I resisted the urge to cross my heart and hope to die. I was afraid Cathryn might take me at my word.

Her lips tightened, and she sighed. "I know this seems extreme to you both, and I seem unreasonable, but at the moment, more than ever, we need to make sure our people are protected. It's not just a matter of business. It can mean life or death." She blinked again, and her fingers worried at the hem of her blouse. It hit me that I was seeing Cathryn's tells, her nerves. She seemed to be in utter control all the time. I began to wonder what had happened to upset her beyond Lucas's so-called indiscretion.

"Okay, she's promised. Can we get on with it now? Can you tell us what you found out?"

Cathryn leaned down to pull out her tablet. She clicked it on and ran her fingers over the screen. "It took me a long time to track down some of this because it's part of the new normal Carruthers has lately been facing."

At my look of confusion, she shifted on the sofa. "Carruthers is my family company. As I think Lucas has shared, we work with people who have extraordinary gifts, so very little surprises me. We've dealt with all sorts of talents over the years. But lately. . .we've been made aware that there is perhaps a larger picture. More to the world than what even we anticipated. There are forces that have competing goals. You might even consider them to be on the side of. . .evil."

Lucas was watching her intently, and his fingers tightened around mine. "Do you think what happened to me is part of that?"

Cathryn's eyes flicked between the two of us. "We think it's connected, perhaps, but it doesn't mean that you yourself are evil, Lucas. Given the note left for you, it seems that this was not a random occurrence. You weren't just happened upon."

"But what happened to me, Cathryn? How did I become a death broker, and what else am I?"

"As far as our researching team could tell—and please know, this is all new to us, too—death brokers are born to the role. In other words, this was nothing you did. This was something you were always fated to become."

"Fate is a tricky thing." Lucas frowned as he murmured the words. When I cast him a questioning glance, he shook his head. "It was in the note." He turned back to Cathryn. "Speaking of the note, did you make any headway into finding out who this Veronica is?"

Cathryn's eyes slid away from ours. "Nothing conclusive. Now. . ." She flipped several pages on the screen of her tablet. "On the idea of vampires, of course, I was met with some opposition from my team. Some of them refused to even look into it. And there is so much lore that it's not easy to separate what's real from what's genuine." She clicked off the tablet and slid it back into her bag. "I had to step outside our normal sources to get any information at all. And what I found is that apparently some of the symptoms you described to me are consistent with vampirism. Not all of them, and there are some mentioned that you haven't experienced."

"So what does it mean? Am I a vampire or not?"

Cathryn lifted her shoulders. "Our best guess is that you're a half-vampire. You didn't die. You were transformed. You need to consume blood, but not exclusively. Sunlight and garlic bother you, but they don't harm you. Are you seeing the trend?"

"What about immortality?" I spoke up at last.

"We don't know. As I said, all of this is conjecture, based on questionable information. My feeling is that you'll be discovering the truth as you go along. On our side, we'll continue to investigate. That's all I can tell you."

Lucas exhaled. "Okay. Well. . .I guess it's confirmation, if nothing else. I'm not crazy, right?"

Cathryn smiled a little. "Not any more than you were before. Oh, I did have another thought. You'd told me last time I was here that it was difficult for you to be around people because of the numbers you keep hearing. What our sources tell us is that there is always a time of training and transition, and I have a hunch that your impromptu vamping interfered with that process. Most of the time, brokers are taught how to handle the voices. You missed out on that. But happily for you, I know someone who can help you there. She's on staff at Carruthers, and she'd be glad to talk with you." She handed a small white card to Lucas.

"Thanks. I've got to learn to deal with the numbers if I'm ever going out in the world again."

"I'm curious about one thing. You told me that you didn't hear Jackie's numbers when you met her."

He smiled at me. "Yeah, that's right. I never have." He frowned. "I didn't hear yours either, Cat. Not when you were here before, and not today."

"Hmm. Fascinating." The dry tone of her voice belied the word. "Likely the reason you didn't hear mine had to do with my blocking power. I keep up powerful boundaries to keep anything supernatural from getting in. Now, is there anything else different about Jackie as she pertains to you?"

Lucas glanced at me, and I felt my face grow warm. "Uh. . .yes. But I think it falls more in the vampire area than the broker."

"If you don't tell me everything, I can't help you." Cathryn smiled again, this time with thin lips.

"I want her blood." He was blunt. "I don't care about anyone else's blood. I can drink the bagged stuff without a problem. But Jackie's is different. And it seems like it's connected to. . .intimacy."

"I see." Cathryn's lips just about disappeared this time. "That doesn't seem to be a typical situation either. There is, apparently, a strain of vampirism wherein the vampire only craves the blood of the evil. Have you experienced that?"

Lucas shook his head. "Not to the best of my knowledge. Either I haven't run across someone evil or I don't have that strain."

Cathryn tilted her head. "Unless Jackie has something to hide."

Before I could open my mouth to respond, Lucas jumped up. "Cathryn, stop. I get that you're mad at me, and I get that we have. . .history. But I'm going to remind you, Cat, you're the one who told me we wouldn't work. I didn't dump you. I'm not saying I think you were wrong, but you don't have any right to be snide now. And you won't be rude or hurtful to Jackie. She doesn't deserve it."

Cathryn's face didn't change but hurt flashed in those ice-blue eyes. "I understand." She turned her head just a little to look at me. "I apologize, Jackie. That was rude and uncalled-for."

"It's okay." The air around us was so charged that it felt heavy. I couldn't stay there any longer. I stood up. "Lucas, I'm going home. If there's nothing else you'd like me to hear, I think I should. . ." I wracked my brain for a good excuse to leave. "I should go check on Mrs. Mac." I pivoted on my heel. "Cathryn, lovely to see you again. Have a safe trip back home. Lucas, I'll talk to you later."

I made it through the front door without falling flat on my face this time. I'd just stepped off the porch when I heard Cathryn calling my name.

She stood on the step and closed the door behind her. "Jackie, could I please have a moment?"

I managed a nod.

She licked her lips and turned her head to look out over the grass, not meeting my eyes. "You don't know me at all. But I am a woman who lives by precision. In my line of work, being in control is essential. My people, those who work for me, they can afford the luxury of wild passions and impetuousness. I cannot. Lives depend on me being clear-headed. If I didn't know that before, I certainly learned it this year." She closed her eyes, and her hand reached to grip the railing. I opened my mouth to warn her that it was rickety, but she seemed to realize it and let go.

"This summer, when I met Lucas, I was in a very vulnerable place. For the first time ever, I opened myself to someone who had the potential to hurt me. Do you know, Lucas was the first person who ever gave me a nickname? I abhor them. I only use given names, and I don't tolerate anyone calling me anything except Cathryn. But he began to call me Cat, and when I was with him, I *was* Cat."

I saw her softening as she remembered, and sympathy filled my heart. She scowled.

"I realized shortly after I returned to Florida that I'd made a mistake. I like Lucas. He's a wonderful man, with enormous intelligence and a great capacity for compassion. But the person he met in Cape May cannot exist in Florida. Not if I want to do my job."

I didn't know what to say to her. "I'm sorry you feel that way, Cathryn. It must be very difficult for you."

"Please don't feel sorry for me. I'm not telling you this to make you feel bad. I hope you'll accept my apology for what I said inside. It was very unlike me."

I nodded. "I do accept it. You don't know me either, but I

only want the best for Lucas, too. You and I are very different people, but I hope that we can get along. For his sake, if nothing else. He really does still care for you. I don't want to get in the middle of that."

Cathryn didn't answer for a minute. She seemed to be listening to some voice I couldn't hear. Finally, she sighed. "I appreciate that. A lot of women wouldn't like their boyfriends maintaining ties with an old fling."

"I'm not sure we're in a place yet where I'd call Lucas my boyfriend. It's all very new. And considering all the complications, it feels like nothing is normal with us."

"You'd be surprised at how committed Lucas already is to you. I don't think you have anything to worry about." She met my eyes finally, and I saw acceptance. "I'll let you go now. Thanks for listening."

Cathryn turned to go back into the house, her back straight and her steps precise. I thought she looked very alone.

Chapter 9

IT WAS STANDING-room-only at Al's memorial service the next day. St. Crispin's was bursting at the seams, and it gratified me to see how many people had come out to honor this man. Mrs. Mac and I sat in the pew behind the children, at the request of the family. Lucas had opted not to join us for more than one reason.

"I'll hear the numbers for everyone, Jackie. Until I can meet with this woman from Carruthers, I need to limit my exposure to crowds. And what'll happen if I'm called to a Reckoning in the middle of the service? That'd be a little hard to explain to everyone."

I had to agree. I'd explained to Mrs. Mac that Lucas was recovering from an illness and was strictly prohibited from being around large groups of people, per his doctor's orders. She understood and made noises about taking him chicken soup. I made a mental note to nip that in the bud; Mrs. Mac was a wonderful woman, but she'd make Lucas's recovery her life mission and drive him nuts if I let it happen.

The service was beautiful, with eulogies given by two of Al's children and several friends from the community. Father Gonzalez spoke about Al being in a better place, and I smiled, thinking of the beautiful golden light that had flowed from Lucas's eyes that night. I missed my friend keenly, but I was comforted to know he had moved to a new life. I had to believe he was with his beloved wife, and probably with Nana, too.

Mrs. Mac squeezed my hand. As though she were reading my mind, she whispered into my ear, "I can just see him up there playing rummy with Maureen, the two of them arguing as they did. They were such pals."

We all gathered at Leone's afterward for the repast. The staff had outdone themselves, cooking Al's most popular dishes, trays of baked ziti, chicken parmesan, sausage and peppers and eggplant rollatini. I helped them toss salads and sliced endless loaves of crisp Italian bread.

"Doesn't seem right not to have him here, calling out orders and telling us how to do it right." Mary stood next to me, sniffling into her lacy handkerchief.

"He'll always be here, won't he?" I had been studiously avoiding looking at the spot on the floor where Al had fallen. Dena had told me that the police had been reluctant to allow people into the diner, but since they'd exhausted all the crime scene investigation at the restaurant, there'd been no reason to keep the place closed.

"He'd want us to re-open." Mary nodded, agreeing with me. "There should be people here, eating and enjoying themselves. I haven't talked to the children yet to see what they plan to do."

I draped a comforting arm around her shoulder. "They haven't decided yet, but I know they plan to take care of all the staff while they make up their minds. Al would want that, too." I picked up a basket of bread. "I'm going to make the rounds again. We have some new people sitting down now."

I went by all the booths and tables, serving fresh, hot bread. I knew most everyone, and I lingered to chat with a few, sharing memories or just the trite phrases we all fell back on during these times.

A woman I didn't recognize sat alone at the counter. She was older, had dark hair and wide brown eyes, and she didn't speak to anyone as she ate her salad.

"Would you care for some bread?" I used the tongs to offer her a slice.

"Thanks." She took it and dropped it on the side of her plate. She seemed uncomfortable, almost uneasy.

"I don't think I know you. I'm Jackie O'Brien." I set down the bread and extended my hand. "Al was a good friend of mine. How did you know him?"

She regarded my hand for a second and then took it briefly. "Antonia DiBartola. I'm. . .my father knew Al. Many years ago, in New Jersey."

"Oh, it's great you could be here for the service. Do you live down here now?"

Antonia shook her head. "No, I still live in New Jersey. I just happened to be down here visiting my mother." She broke off a piece of bread and looked down at it in her hand. "Everyone says he was such a wonderful man. What the people at the church were saying. . .was it all true?"

I eased my hip onto the stool next to her. "All of it and more. I never knew a better man than Al, and I have the world's best dad and brothers. So that's saying something. Al never failed to help someone who needed it. He took lonely people under his wing. He worked with the homeless shelters, with the church. . .he gave more kids their first jobs than anyone else in the community. Yes, it was all true."

She pushed her plate back. "I didn't know." She murmured the words so low, I had to lean forward to hear them. "I didn't know what he was like now."

"Is your father here, too?" I glanced around, trying to match her to one of the crowds of old men milling around.

"No, he. . .he died a long time ago."

I frowned, confused. Her dad must've known Al a very long time ago. I guessed she was at least thirty years older than me.

"I'm sorry, I have to go." Antonia stood up, nearly knocking me off my stool. "Thanks for the food."

She hiked a heavy black bag onto her shoulder and pushed through the crowd, muttering her excuses. She was out the door before I could even stand.

"Who was that?" Dena was at my elbow, staring after the woman.

"She said her dad knew yours, a long time ago in New Jersey. Her name was Antonia. . .Di-something-or-other. Does it ring a bell?"

"No." She frowned. "Seemed like she was in a hurry to leave."

I shrugged. "Yeah. She asked me if everything she'd heard about Al at the church was true. And when I said it was, she looked shaken."

"Hmmm." Dena shook her head. "People are odd." She slid her arm around my waist and hugged me. "Thanks for all of your help, Jackie. I don't know what we'd have done without everyone down here."

"It's the least I could do. You know how much Al meant to me." I laid my head on her shoulder briefly. "I'm going to miss him so much. Thanks for sharing your dad with me all these years."

"Are you kidding? Thank you for keeping your eye on him all this time. We worried about Dad down here without any of us. Every time we came to visit, we tried to persuade him to sell the diner, come back home and live with one of us. But he never would. He said he had to keep working as long as he could."

"He didn't see it as work. He just saw it as life." I smiled. "Which reminds me. I have all the notes and recipes for the cookbook. I'd like to go ahead and put it together for publication, if you and your family agree. The profits would go to the estate, of course, but I want to make sure that dream is realized."

"Oh, Jackie. You don't know how happy that makes me." She wiped at her eyes. "Definitely. And if you need anything at all for it, any help, please let me know. He was so excited about that book. Seeing it come to life. . .it'll be like holding onto a little part of him. Thank you."

I stayed at the diner to help with clean up after the final guest had departed. Mary and I were the last two out the door, and I caught her staring back into the dark, sadness wreathing her worn face.

"They may keep it open, they may sell it to someone who doesn't change one thing. But it doesn't matter, you know? It'll never be the same. That time is over. The true spirit of Leone's died with Al."

I was still thinking about her words as I unlocked my front door. To my surprise, Makani met me, his little body writhing in joy.

"What are you doing out, baby? Who let you out of your crate?"

"Sorry, that was me." Lucas stepped out of the kitchen, holding a wooden spoon in his hand. "I figured you'd be tired when you got home, so I made you dinner. And I took the pup out for his business, and I fed him, too."

"Go, you." I slipped the black heels off my feet and moaned in pleasure. "God, you have no idea how good that feels. Oh, baby."

Lucas watched me, his mouth hanging slightly open. "Yeah. Oh, baby."

I stuck out my tongue. "Until you've spent almost ten hours in three-inch heels, you have nothing to say, mister." I fell onto the couch with another groan. "My feet hurt, my back hurts. .

.I'm pretty sure not an inch of my body isn't aching."

"Poor thing." Lucas sat on the end of the sofa and put my feet in his lap. He massaged the insteps, using his thumbs until my eyes rolled back into my head.

"Oh, my God, that feels amazing. Never stop. Ever."

"Okay, but then who's going to serve you the best potato soup you've ever eaten?"

"Seriously? You made me potato soup?"

"I did. I can't cook much, but my mom made sure I knew how to make this soup." He patted the tops of my feet. "Stay here, and I'll bring it to you."

"Wash your hands first," I called after him.

"Thanks, mom."

I lay my head back on the arm of the sofa and listened to him in the kitchen, talking to Makani who had trotted in after him. I was exhausted and still sad from the day, but Lucas was taking care of me. He'd made me soup. He'd come over to my house so I didn't have to be alone tonight. And for the first time since Nana died, there was sense of hominess, of family, in my house. Someone else was here, someone who cared about me.

I didn't know whether it was the extreme fatigue or all of the emotions of the past few days, but as I lay there, tears began to stream down my face. I wiped them away with my hand, trying to get rid of the evidence before Lucas came back.

"Jackie, what's wrong?" He stood next to me, carrying a tray that included a bowl of steaming soup that smelled fan-freaking-tastic, a plate with a crusty roll and a glass of my favorite white wine. He had a napkin under the spoon. It was the most beautiful thing I'd ever seen.

"Nothing." I sniffled and reached for the tray. "I'm just tired. This looks amazing."

"I'll be right there, I'm just going to get my bowl." Makani pranced alongside Lucas's feet as he went back to the kitchen.

I tasted my soup and nearly swooned. "This is most definitely the best potato soup I've ever had. You can tell your mom she succeeded."

"Thanks." Lucas took his place on the end of the couch again. "How did everything go today?"

I sighed. "It was hard, but the turnout was beyond what we'd expected. Al's kids were appreciative. And I think everyone in town, possibly everyone in Florida, came back to Leone's for the repast. It was insane."

"I'm sorry I couldn't be there."

I sipped another spoonful of warm potato-y goodness. "It's okay, Lucas. You didn't really know Al. No one expected you to be at the service."

"I would've gone for you."

I laid my spoon in the bowl and set it back on the tray. "Lucas, I appreciate all of this. But you know you don't have to feel sorry for me. And. . .the fact that we share your secrets and we messed around the other night doesn't mean you owe me anything."

"I know all of that. I'm not doing anything because I pity you, Jackie. I'm doing it because I want to." He dipped a piece of bread into his soup. "I know it's been fast between us in some ways, but it's not meaningless. I know you're a little uncertain about where we stand—"

I frowned. "I am?"

Lucas blew out a breath. "Yeah. Cathryn said you were."

"Wait a minute, why would Cathryn tell you that? She referred to you as my boyfriend, and I said that might be a little premature. But I didn't have any deep talk with her about my feelings."

"I think it was something she heard you think." He spoke so matter-of-factly that for a minute I didn't react.

"Something she what now?"

He had the good grace to look guilty. "I guess I forgot to tell you that Cathryn can hear thoughts."

"She *what?*" I nearly dropped my wine glass.

"Yeah, that's her ability. She usually blocks the thoughts,

but I guess she was suspicious about you, so she sort of. . .listened in."

I closed my eyes, running through all the horribly embarrassing things I'd thought the day before. I remembered how she'd looked at me a few times with an odd expression on her face. She must've been hearing things she didn't like.

"How could you not tell me that? Do you know how many mortifying thoughts I probably had today? I'll never be able to look at her again."

"Relax, Jackie. Cathryn's been dealing with this her entire life. She doesn't hold anyone's thoughts against them." Lucas finished his soup and set it down. "The point I was trying to make is that we're friends, you and me. I think we're heading to something more, and I like that. I won't push you too fast, and if I do, just tell me. We'll talk about it."

I leaned back again, regarding the man sitting at my feet. He was in rumpled chic today, wearing khaki shorts that could've used a good ironing—or at least another ten minutes on wrinkle guard in the dryer—along with a black polo that set off his coloring. He'd ditched the contacts for his glasses, and the brown eyes that regarded me through them were steady.

What'd I ever done to deserve this package of kind, sexy and sweet, spiced up with just a hint of the unknown and dangerous? Yet here he was, offering me friendship and more. Everything I'd ever dreamed of was right here, close enough to touch, and all I had to do was reach out and take hold.

I finished my wine and set down the glass. "When I first began to work at the magazine, I met a man named Will. He was in the sales department. He was a little older than me, and he was charming and self-deprecating. Everyone told me how great he was. He didn't give me the hard sell, though. He took me under his wing, helped me get to know people at work. You know, it was my first time in the big city, and he wanted to make sure I was okay. And then he started suggesting stuff we could do on weekends together. I introduced him to my parents, my brothers,

Leesa. . .everyone loved him. They all said I'd found the perfect guy for me.

"Will proposed to me in front of the whole staff at our Christmas party two years after I'd started at the magazine. Everyone was in on it, and my parents were there, and Nana. . .Nonna, my grandmother on my mom's side, had passed away that year, and Will had her ring re-set and resized for me, and that's what he used as my engagement ring. So that she could be part of it too, he said."

Lucas didn't say anything, but he reached over to take my foot into his lap again.

"My mom went into major wedding planning mode. We set up a big church wedding, because of course Will was Catholic, too, and they reserved a reception hall on the river. We were going to get married at five o'clock and then the reception would begin with cocktails overlooking the Hudson as the sun set. I had six bridesmaids, and two huge wedding showers.

"The day of the last fitting for my gown, I came out of the bridal shop and started walking back to the magazine. A woman stopped me and asked if I'd give her a minute. She said she knew Will, and she thought we should talk."

The hand rubbing my foot tightened. He had an inkling of what was coming.

"The long sordid story short is that Will was married. He'd met this girl when they were in college, she'd gotten pregnant, and they got married. She still lived in the same little town where they'd gone to college. They had three children. One of them had been conceived and born while I was dating Will.

"According to Will's wife, he kept them in this little town because he traveled for work so much, and she hated the city. He'd go home once or twice a month for a few days—of course, that was when I thought he was traveling for work. And I'm pretty sure he planned to keep it up, to maintain this double life. But his wife's sister happened to be traveling, stopped in my hometown for lunch, picked up a copy of my mom's newspaper and saw a picture of Will and me taken after one of the wedding showers. That's how the wife found out."

Lucas stared at me with narrowed eyes. "He posed for pictures for a newspaper? Was he stupid or incredibly cocky?" He ran his hand up my calf and squeezed. "I mean, I'm just saying. Obviously the guy's a dick, but he must've had cojones the size of an elephant's to think he could get away with it."

"Yeah, that's the truth. He honestly didn't see it as a problem. When I confronted him, crying and shaking, he brushed it aside. I was making a big deal out of nothing. He'd get a quickie divorce before our big day—those are the actual words he used, believe it or not—and it'd all be fine. He didn't see his wife as an issue at all."

Lucas exhaled, shaking his head. "What did you do?"

"I did what I had to do. I called it all off. I told my mom and dad, and they took care of everything on their end. My mother asked me how I wanted to handle it: she'd just tell people we'd changed our minds, or she'd tell them the truth. I decided go big or go home. So she actually did an article in her newspaper and exposed the whole thing.

"What hurt the most was that I felt humiliated at work. I tried to quit the magazine, but my editor absolutely refused. She said why the hell would I allow this asshole to chase me from doing what I loved? And she was right. They fired his lying ass and sent him slinking back to Podunk. A year later, I got the column, and I moved to Florida."

"So you're telling me all this to say me being a death broker and a half-vamp looks pretty damn good compared to your ex-fiancé with a wife?"

I laughed. "Yeah, I guess. I wanted you to know where I'm coming from. Will was the one and only romantic relationship in my life. The scars he left were nasty, but they're healed. My experience with him made me a lot more. . .selective about who I date."

Lucas laid his hand over his heart. "I promise I have no wife or children hiding anywhere. I've never been married. I came close to being engaged to my college girlfriend, but it didn't work out, and that was a good thing, for both of us. Other than that, I've been a serial dater. Casual stuff, nothing serious." He leaned closer to me. "Maybe I was waiting for the right one."

"Maybe." I reached to touch his face, smiling when he turned his lips to kiss my palm. "Do you believe in fate, Lucas? The sort of thing Cathryn was taking about, I mean. Do you think it really was your fate to be a death broker?"

"I've always been on the fence about the whole fate deal, but I can tell you no one gave me the choice in being a broker. I didn't interview for the job." He pulled my feet, dragging me down the couch until I was draped over his lap. He slid one hand beneath the hem of my dress where it had hiked up on my leg. "But I don't want to talk about fate anymore, unless it's how I'm meant to find out what you have on under your dress."

I scooted closer and linked my hands behind his neck. "I think that's a sure thing, buddy. I mean, potato soup, fresh bread and wine? *And* a foot rub? You're golden."

"Good, because I've been in a perpetual state of want since I got called away the other night." He grasped the dress and pulled it over my head, making me giggle when the neck caught on my ear.

"Smooth, baby, real smooth." I untangled the material and tossed the dress over the back of the sofa, shaking free my hair.

"Are you naked? Or just about?" Lucas cupped my boobs, rubbing the nipples through the lace of my bra. "Then mission accomplished."

I slung one leg across his thighs and straddled him. "I think tonight it's my turn to give orders. So take off the shirt." I helped him and then leaned down to kiss the top of one pec. "And the shorts, too." I rose up to give him room to shuck them off. When I sank back down, his hard length rubbed against the juncture of my legs, separated only by the cotton of his boxers and the lace of my underwear.

"I hope you put up the do-not-disturb sign, because if you get called to a Reckoning in the next half hour, there's going to be some very surprised advocates." I covered his flat nipples with my hands, letting the hard nubs drill into my palms before I bent to cover them with my mouth. Lucas groaned.

"If I get called in the next thirty minutes, there's going to be some very choice words spoken. God, that feels good."

"Mmmm." I worked my way down until I knelt on the floor in front of him. Keeping my eyes on his, I hooked the waistband of his boxers and slid them down his legs. His cock jutted up, hard and long and demanding my attention. I was happy to oblige.

I took him in my hand, stroking up and down. I held him at the base and circled the head with my thumb before I leaned up to take him into my mouth.

Lucas threaded his fingers through my hair, moaning words I couldn't quite understand. I figured most of them were along the lines of 'don't stop' and 'oh God, oh God, oh God.' I moved down further, slowly bringing in more of his hard length until the head touched the back of my throat. I swallowed, and he groaned my name.

I hollowed my cheeks as I brought my mouth back up, surrounding him with the suction at the same time that I used my tongue to stroke. His hips began to piston as my rhythm increased.

"Jackie—" He pulled at my hair. "Get up here. I want to be inside you when I come."

I was loath to stop what I was doing, but Lucas hauled me up, bringing my lips to his and kissing me open-mouthed, his tongue plunging in to tangle with mine. He broke away just long enough to whisper into my ear.

"My wallet's in the pocket of my shorts—condom in there— can you get it?"

Instead of answering, I leaned away to fumble for his shorts. My hand closed on his wallet, and I gave it to him. When he found the small foil packet, I took it and tore it open with my teeth, rolling the rubber sheath over him.

"Jackie—let me touch you." He spread his fingers over me as I lifted up over him. "God, you're so wet."

I wrapped my fingers around his. "My show this time, re-member?" I positioned him at my entrance, and with my eyes still fastened on Lucas's, I lowered myself, impaling myself on his cock.

He growled, gripping my hips and bringing my breasts to his mouth. He sucked one turgid nipple between his lips, over the lace, using his teeth to worry it and make me cry out. I ground myself against him, seeking friction at the right spot.

"God, you feel so good. So tight on me. Just—ahhhh." He shifted, and that tiny bit of difference made him stroke my interi-or walls in the precise point that sent me over the edge. I arched my back, pulsing around him.

As I floated down from the peak, Lucas flipped me onto the sofa on my back. Kneeling between my legs, he licked me hard once, his tongue setting fire to my sensitive sex. He sucked the small knob of nerves into his mouth, using the tip of tongue to rub up and down. As I lifted my hips to get closer to him, he replaced his mouth with his fingers, and I felt the briefest burn of his teeth on my skin, the undeniably sensuous feeling of him sucking there, humming as I came again.

And then he was above me again, plunging into me, hard and fast and calling my name. I didn't think I could possibly get any higher, until his fingers covered me, pinching my clit as he slid inside me. I bucked toward him, and Lucas froze over me, muscles tensed as he ground out my name one last time.

He fell onto the couch next to me, both of us breathing hard in a tangle of sweat-covered limbs. I rolled just enough to lay my head against his chest, smiling at the pounding of his heart.

"Thank you, thank you, thank you." Lucas murmured the words, and I laughed.

"No thanks necessary. I think I'm the one who needs to be

expressing gratitude."

"Well, I definitely appreciate you, don't get me wrong, but I was mostly saying thanks to whatever powers transport me to a Reckoning. If I'd gotten called in the middle of that, someone was going to pay."

"I'm with you." I curled around him, and he slid his arm beneath me, pulling me tighter.

"Can I stay tonight?" He sounded a little hesitant, and I smiled against the slick skin of his chest.

"I think that can be arranged. That is, unless you're rushing off to clean your andirons or something."

His body shook as he laughed. "No andirons. You have to admit, running off to determine the final destination of a soul is a much better excuse than andirons."

Chapter 10

"**I**'M GOING TO write Al's cookbook." I was lying on my back, with Lucas's head on my stomach. Neither of us had anything pressing this morning, so we could afford to sleep in a little. Lucas had been called to a Reckoning just after midnight. I was vaguely aware when he transported away, and when he came back, he woke me up in the most pleasant way possible. We'd both fallen back to sleep after.

"Good. I think he'd want that."

"Yeah, me too. I checked it out with Dena, and she's thrilled. I'm going to work on that today." I ran my fingers through Lucas's hair. "I just don't know who I can get to be my taste tester."

I felt his smile against my skin. "Does it have garlic?"

"It's Italian food. What do you think?"

"Maybe you need to enlist Mrs. Mac."

"Or maybe I need to find a boyfriend who's not allergic to garlic." I froze for a minute, my hand still on his head. I hadn't meant to use the b-word. Even after our discussion last night, I was leery of assuming too much too soon.

"Isn't it enough to have a boyfriend who gives you five orgasms a night?"

I grinned, relief filling me. "I guess you might have a point." I resumed stroking his head. "So what're your plans for the day?"

He moved his shoulder in what I assumed was a shrug. "Writing. Research. I'll probably call that chick from Carruthers to set up an appointment. Would you want to ride up there with me when I go?"

I bit the side of my lip. "Depending on when, sure. Though I'm not sure how happy Cathryn would be about that."

"She'll be cool, I promise." He closed his eyes. "Mmm, that feels good."

"What're you writing about? If it's okay for me to ask."

"Of course it is. I have no secrets from you." He picked up my other hand from where it lay at my side and kissed my knuckles. "I was going to write an epic Civil War family story. You know, generations, brother against brother, all that. But given everything I've experienced in the last few months, I'm thinking of maybe trying to write paranormal. What do you think?"

"I think it's a good idea. Lots of inspiration in your life. I can't wait to read what you come up with."

Lucas rolled over and put his feet on the floor. "I guess I should get started." He glanced back over shoulder at me. "Are you getting up?"

I stretched, yawning. "Yep. I was thinking of making French toast. No garlic. Any one you know who might be interested in that?"

Lucas leaned over me and dropped a kiss on my lips. "That's definitely a dish I can get behind. You cook, I'll take pup duty."

Lucas and I fell into a rhythm with very little effort. Most nights we ate at my house, since that was where the food lived. After dinner, we took Makani for a walk around the block and then came back to sit on the porch. Some nights, we watched movies or just sat on the sofa talking.

More often than not, Lucas was called to a Reckoning at some point during our evening or in the middle of the night. I joked that it was like sleeping with a doctor who never knew when he might have to go into the hospital for a patient. Lucas rolled his eyes.

"True, except the docs are making the big bucks. If I'm getting a paycheck for this gig, they've been sending it to the wrong address."

We had breakfast together nearly every morning, unless one of us had an appointment. We took turns cooking, though Lucas's culinary expertise was limited to omelets.

"You and Lucas seem to be getting pretty cozy." Mrs. Mac had stopped over for coffee one morning after Lucas had gone home to work.

I smiled. "I thought that's what you wanted. All you interfering matchmakers."

"Oh, honey, I'm thrilled. The boy seems a little odd to me sometimes, but I guess that's because he's one of those creative types, isn't it?"

"Probably." I sipped my coffee. "He's pretty wonderful, Mrs. Mac. I think Nana would've liked him, don't you?"

She covered my hand. "Jackie, sweetie, all Maureen wanted was for you to be happy. She'd be tickled."

We were both quiet for a moment, remembering, and then Mrs. Mac cleared her throat. "Of course, I won't say I haven't noticed that he leaves here most mornings in the same clothes he wore to your house the night before. I'm not going to tell you how to live your life, but remember what they say about the cow and getting the milk."

I flushed. "Mrs. Mac. Really. And don't you dare say anything to Lucas about cows and milk, do you hear? We're getting along very well. I don't need any interference."

Lucas came over early that afternoon. "I finally nailed down a date to see the psychologist at Carruthers. Can you ride up with me tomorrow morning?"

I was in the middle of staging photos for my column. "Uh, sure, I guess. Kind of last minute, isn't it?"

He nodded. "I guess she's on call for the Carruthers agents quite a bit. She set aside three hours for me tomorrow." He leaned down to scoop up Makani, giving him a rough pet. "I hope she can help me. Seems like a long ride for an iffy situation."

"Think positive." I bumped my shoulder against his. Movement outside the window caught my eye, and I smiled. "Oh, look, Nichelle's here. Let me see if I can catch her before she hauls that cooler to your door."

The blood delivery woman and I had gotten to be friends over the past weeks. I handed off as many cookbooks to her as she wanted, and she gave me feedback on my columns. I was surprised to see her today; I knew the baby was due any way, and she'd planned to stop working deliveries until after maternity leave.

"Nichelle!" I called her name as she bent into the back seat of her car. "Hey there, you crazy woman. What're you doing here?"

When she turned around, I saw that her face was red, and her forehead was dotted with perspiration. "Delivery. One. . .last. . .delivery." Each word came out in a tiny puff of breath as though she were toting a heavy load. But she didn't have anything in her hands.

"My God, Nichelle, are you in labor?" I yelled the words. "What the hell are you doing?"

She leaned against the car, pressing her back against the door. "I started feeling contractions this afternoon. I was planning to go to the hospital, but Lucas's package was late getting in. I wanted to wait for it. I figured I could drop it on the way."

She bared her teeth, breath hissing. "This one's coming faster than the other two. Oh, my God, George is going to kill me."

George, I knew, was her husband, the man who'd been nagging her to stop working a month ago. He swore she'd end up giving birth at a delivery stop. The man must've been psychic.

"Who should I call?" I glanced around, hoping that Lucas had followed me out. But being a man, he tended to give the pregnant lady a lot of room. "You can't drive. Here." I stood next to her and pulled her arm over my shoulder. "I'll get you to my car and drive you over to the hospital."

"Okay."

We began walking across the grass toward my driveway, two women doing a clumsy approximation of the three-legged race. We'd gotten a few steps from my car when Nichelle cried out and doubled over. A gush of liquid soaked my feet, and I gritted my teeth against the bile rising in my stomach. *Eww.*

"I can't wait! I gotta stop." She squatted on the ground next to me and began making the most god-awful grunting sound I'd ever heard. I stared at her, horrified.

"For the love of God, Nicelle! You can't have that baby here on my lawn. Come on, get up. We're almost to the car."

But Nicelle was lost in some world that my voice couldn't penetrate. She growled low in her throat, and I saw her face turn even redder. I'd seen my share of soap operas and medical dramas, and it dawned on me that she was pushing. The fool was pushing her baby out, right here in my yard.

"*Lucas!*" I screamed his name, and he flew out the door, his eyes wild. Those same eyes went wide with shock when he caught sight of his blood delivery woman on the ground.

"What the hell is she doing?" His voice was belligerent.

"Pretty sure she's giving birth." *Duh.*

"Well, tell her to stop it! She can't do that here." If I were alarmed by this turn of events, Lucas was downright panicked.

"I think it's too late for that." Some semblance of calm had come over me. "Call 911 and tell them what's happening. And then. . .I take it you don't know anything about delivering a baby?"

His face told me that answer loud and clear.

"Fine. After you call, go get Mrs. Mac. She used to be a nurse."

Lucas disappeared around the front of the house, cell phone in hand as he walked. I shook my head. *Men.* And then I knelt next to the woman at my feet.

"Nichelle, honey, can you get up so I can get you into the house? You don't want to have the baby here."

"No." She was still growling. "It's coming now. Now!" The last word was a shriek, and her hands moved between her knees as she curled her body in on itself. I managed to lower her to the grass and take position in time to catch the slimy, screaming bundle of new human that shot into my hands moments later.

By the time that Mrs. Mac and Lucas arrived, I had Nichelle's new son wrapped in my T-shirt, holding him against chest. A small crowd had gathered a respectful distance away, drawn by the commotion.

Lucas took in the situation and gallantly peeled off his own shirt, shielding me in my pink lace bra from inquiring eyes. The ambulance screeched in moments later, and I was pathetically grateful to hand over baby and mama to the EMTs.

"You were amazing." Lucas circled his arms around me. "How did you know what to do?"

"I didn't do anything but catch him." I leaned back against his chest, suddenly exhausted. "Nichelle did all the work."

A large man with a shaved head pulled up and ran to Nichelle. George, I assumed. He kissed her, examined his new son, and then turned to Lucas and me.

"Thank you so much. I knew this was going to happen, since she won't ever listen to reason—" He leveled a glare at his wife. "But I'm glad it happened here, where she had friends to make sure she was okay. Thank you for taking care of them." He grasped my hand and pumped it.

As they began to move Nichelle and the baby toward the ambulance, she beckoned to me. I leaned over to hear what she was saying.

"We're naming the baby Jack, in honor of you." She paused and a hopeful gleam shone in her eye. "Just think. This little adventure would make a wonderful column: *How I Delivered My Boyfriend's Blood Supplier's Baby.*"

Chapter 11

WE WERE ON the road the next morning, bright and early, heading north to where the Carruthers headquarters was located. I drove, since I had my reservations about what could happen if Lucas were transported to a Reckoning when he was behind the wheel.

About an hour into the trip, my phone buzzed. Lucas retrieved it from my purse and handed me the headset. I frowned when I saw the name on the screen.

"Dena, hi. How're you doing?" I hadn't talked with Al's daughter since the day of the memorial service. I'd sent her a few email updates on the cookbook's progress; we'd found a photographer, and I was slowly making my way through the recipes.

"Jackie, I'm sorry for bothering you. But we've come across a sort of troubling situation here, and I need your input."

The police still hadn't solved the mystery of Al's murder. I knew they were leaning toward calling it a botched robbery, claiming that the perpetrator had gotten scared off after he shot

Al. I wasn't buying it. I wondered if Dena's troubling situation had anything to do with that.

"Of course. You know anything I can do, I'm more than happy to help."

She sighed, and I could almost feel her worry. "We've been going through Dad's paperwork and accounts. You know, all the estate mess. He's done a wonderful job of keeping everything in order, but there is one entry that we can't figure out. Dad was making a monthly payment, a fairly large one. The accountant can't tell us why or for what—he just sent the cashiers check—but he did say it's been going on as long as he worked for Dad."

A vague uneasiness filled me. "Do you have copies of the checks? A way to trace where the payments were going?"

"Yes. They went to a woman named Lucinda DiBartola. The address is a PO box in New Jersey."

"DiBartola." The name rang a bell. I thought for a few minutes before it clicked. "Dena, remember the woman at the repast? The one who I was sitting with at the counter? I'm almost positive that was her last name. But her first name was Antonia."

Dena was silent for a few beats. "Jackie, I don't know what to think. My dad. . .you know what he was like. But why would he be sending this woman money for years without telling any of us about it?"

"I don't know." I had some pretty good ideas, but I didn't want to link any of them with Al, my friend. "Listen, Dena, let me do some poking around down here. That woman said her mother lived around us. I bet I can dig her up and figure out what's going on." I paused. "Try not to let this upset you, okay? I'm sure it's nothing. You know your father. He wouldn't do anything wrong."

"I'm trying to hold onto that thought. But sometimes when a person isn't around to defend himself, it's easy to build monsters."

I tried to reassure her again before we hung up. Once I'd pulled out my ear buds, Lucas took them from me. "That didn't sound good."

I ran down the gist of the conversation with her. Lucas winced. "You know what it sounds like, don't you?"

I cast him a sideways look. "You think Al had another child, don't you? Outside his marriage. One the others didn't know about."

"I didn't know him well, Jackie. Maybe I'm way off base."

I shook my head. "No, it was my first thought, too. I don't think Al liked to keep secrets, but if he thought he was protecting his family, he'd absolutely do it." I glanced into the rearview mirror and changed lanes. "Do you think it had something to do with his murder?"

Lucas wrinkled his brow. "I doubt it. I mean, if he was making these payments all those years, why would someone cut off that source of money?"

"Yeah, I guess you're right." The navigation on my phone instructed me that my destination was ahead on the right. I peered into the trees around us. "Is this place a tree house? I don't see anything else."

"There's a road, Cathryn said. . .there it is."

I braked and made the turn, but barely. We drove down a narrow road that opened to a huge house, surrounded by acres of manicured gardens. The round driveway curved in front of the door, and I stopped the car on the side.

"Wow." Lucas stepped out of the car, and I walked around to join him. "This is some place."

"You must be Lucas." The door had opened, and a small woman with multi-colored hair stood watching us. "Come in, come in, my dears. So lovely to meet you at last."

We followed her into a cavernous entry hall. "I'm Zoe. I'm excited to meet you, Lucas, and of course, you too, Jackie." She beamed at us with such joy that I almost thought sunbeams were going to shoot out her fingertips. "Now, we have a lot of work to do. Jackie, I know you've made this long drive up here to keep dear Lucas company, but it will be far easier for us to accomplish our work if we're alone."

I nodded. "I figured that. Is there some place I can sit down out of the way?" I lifted my bag. "Have laptop, will work."

"Oh, yes. Go straight down this hallway and turn left when you can't walk any further. There's a small library and conference room to your right. No one will bother you there."

Lucas squeezed my hand. "You'll be okay?"

"Sure. I can take care of myself. Go figure out how to stop hearing voices, you crazy man, you."

The library was exactly where Zoe had pointed it out, down a hallway of gleaming dark wood. I opened the door and settled myself at a table, pulling out my laptop and delving into the text for next week's column. I'd worked for about fifteen minutes before I heard a noise.

"Hello." A voice at the door broke into my concentration. I looked up to see a young woman regarding me with curiosity.

"Hi." I didn't know whether I should stand up and offer to leave or introduce myself. The woman had long black hair that formed a cloud around the translucent skin of her face. Her eyes were a startling blue, out of sync with the rest of her coloring, but all the more attractive for that. She reminded me of a jungle cat, standing almost preternaturally still as she watched me.

"What are you doing here?" The tone was more curiosity than animosity.

"I. . ." As far as I knew, Lucas's visit here wasn't a secret, but Cathryn was so into discretion that I didn't want to break any of her rules. "I'm here with a friend. He's meeting with Zoe."

At the mention of Zoe's name, her face settled into friendlier lines. "Oh." She stared a moment more before she came into the room, moving with the same feline grace. "I'm Nell." She offered a small white hand.

"I'm Jackie." I shook her hand, smiling. "Do you work here?"

She inclined her head. "I guess I do. Yes."

I searched for something else to say. "I know Cathryn. She's a friend of my boyfriend's." I'd been experimenting with that word for the last few weeks. It was getting easier to use.

Nell's face broke into a smile, transforming from merely arresting to downright gorgeous. "Really? Cathryn? I didn't know she had any friends, outside maybe Zoe and Harley."

"Nell, where did you go? Oh." The guy who came around the corner was tall, dark and if I'd been ten years younger, I'd have termed him yummy. His eyes skimmed over me in surprise before fastening on Nell with an expression that told me all I needed to know.

"I came in to get a book." She smiled at him. "This is Jackie. Her friend is having a session with Zoe."

"Ah. Lucky friend." He winked at me and took a step forward. "I'm Rafe Brooks. I work here." He slid his hand into Nell's. "We both do."

"Jackie knows Cathryn." Nell grinned up at Rafe, who shook his head.

"I think Nell and I make Cathryn's life a little more exciting than she'd like." He looked down at Nell again. "Let's not disturb Jackie any more than we have. I found the book in the other library. I was about to tell you that, but when I turned around, you'd disappeared into thin air."

She rolled her eyes. "Not quite. I haven't mastered that one yet." She glanced back at me as Rafe pulled her hand. "Nice to meet you, Jackie. I'm sure we'll see you again."

As they turned down the hallway, I heard Rafe's voice. "I'm never sure what you can and cannot do at any given moment. I wouldn't put it past you to just learn to vanish one day."

Nell laughed, a low, throaty sound. "Keeping you on your toes is my number one goal."

I tried to go back to work, but there were too many distractions, even in this room. Out the window, I could see people moving around the grounds, driving in golf carts and pulling into and out of a small parking lot in the rear. Before too long, the enticing aroma that I recognized as roast beef began wafting down the hallway.

There was a knock at the door, and a woman in a gray uniform carried in a tray. "Zoe told us you were working in here, and that you might appreciate lunch." She removed the silver dome, revealing a white plate overflowing with food. She set a goblet of ice water down next to it.

"Thank you." I picked up the napkin from the tray and lay it on my lap. "This is an unexpected pleasure."

The woman nodded. "You're very welcome. Just leave the tray outside the door when you're finished."

The food was delicious, and once I'd finished it, I had a hard time staying awake. When Lucas found me an hour later, I was nearly dozing.

"Hey, you ready to go?" He tugged on a lock of my hair.

"Yes. . .although I'm kind of thinking of moving in here. Did you have lunch?"

He laughed. "Yeah, Zoe and I ate in her office. Pretty good, huh?"

We walked out to the car, and Lucas opened the door for me. "I'll drive back."

I glanced at him, surprised. "Is that safe? What if you zap out?"

Lucas smiled. "Zoe and I worked on that. She taught me how to delay a transport. Also. . .I can block the voices now." His voice was gleeful. "She's a miracle worker."

"All that in one session?" I raised my eyebrows as he climbed into the driver's seat.

"Yes, but I'm going to come back. Just to make sure I'm adjusting well to all the changes."

"Awesome. Can you make sure we come back on roast beef days?"

"Ha. Not sure about that, but guess what I'm going to do tonight?"

I smiled big. "This sounds promising. Does it have anything to do with getting naked?"

"You're insatiable. No, I'm going to take you to dinner. Out to a real dinner, with real live people around us. And I'm going to relax while we're there, because I won't worry about transporting or hearing voices. How does that sound?"

I laid my head against the seat. "That sounds fabulous. Still interested in the getting naked part, though. Not gonna lie."

"That's my girl."

Chapter 12

THE DAY AFTER our trip to see Zoe, I had lunch at Leone's. The diner had reopened with the blessing of Al's family, who hadn't yet decided whether they would sell it or keep it. The managers and wait staff were working hard to make sure the restaurant carried on Al's high standards of food and service, and it made my heart happy.

Mary brought me a glass of water and a plate of bread. "So good to see you sitting in your regular spot, Jackie. We've missed you."

"I've missed you all, too." I pointed across from me. "Do you have a minute to sit down?"

She grinned and took the seat. "For you, always. Isn't that what Al used to say?"

I nodded. "All the time." I sipped my water and glanced at her. "Mary, do you know a Lucinda DiBartola?"

Mary leaned back, rolling her shoulders. "Sure. She lives in Windy Glades, just ten minutes down the road. She came from up north, too."

"Did she know Al?"

She pursed her lips. "I don't know. She didn't come in here that I can remember. I only know her from St. Anthony's. We're both in that parish." Mary leaned forward. "Though she lives with this guy. . .Eddie Cortini. . .he's not her husband. They've been together for a long time, but he's never done the right thing by her."

I frowned. "Does she have a daughter? There was a girl at Al's repast named Antonia DiBartola."

"I don't know Lucinda that well, but I've never heard of a daughter. Name isn't that common though. Could be. I've never seen her at Mass with anyone but Eddie."

I left the diner an hour later, with a full stomach and a little more information than I'd had going in. I called Lucas to let him know I was taking a ride down the coast, looking up an old friend. I didn't say she was a friend of mine, but I had a hunch we had a mutual acquaintance.

Thanks to the age of technology and smart phones, I was able to find a listing for Eddie Cortini. He lived in a townhouse two blocks off the beach. I parked on the street and knocked on the front door, butterflies dancing in my stomach. The chances that I was going to find out good news here were pretty low. I wondered if I were ready to learn that Al wasn't quite the man I'd thought.

The woman who answered the door was short, with white hair and snapping black eyes. She looked me up and down, frowning.

"We don't need any cable or security systems here. And you should know, missy, solicitation is strictly forbidden in this complex. You're lucky I don't take you down, turn you in."

I held up my hand. "I'm not soliciting, I promise. Ms. DiBartola?"

The eyes narrowed. "Who's asking?"

The suspicion ran deep in this one. "I think maybe we have a mutual friend. I don't want anything. I just want to talk with you."

"Okay, talk." She folded her arms over her chest.

I sighed. An invitation inside was not forthcoming, clearly. "Alfonso Leone. Did you know him?" I watched her face closely for any sign of recognition.

Her forehead wrinkled. "Leone? The name sounds familiar, but. . .oh, wait, he was the old man who was killed in Palm Dunes, right? Sad, very sad. Did they ever find the crazy who did it?"

I shook my head. "Not yet."

"So bad things are getting. If I had grandchildren, believe me, I'd be on top of them all the time, no going off by themselves. It's not safe anywhere anymore. I used to cry and cry because my daughter didn't have children, but now, I'm not so unhappy."

I leaned forward. "You have a daughter?"

"Sure, my Antonia. She's a big-shot lawyer up in New Jersey, but she comes to visit, two, three times a year. She's one of these who married her job, you know?"

"Sure." I nodded. "You and your husband must be very proud of her."

"Oh, Eddie here, he's not her father. No, Antonia's father. . ." Lucinda's face softened into lines of old grief. "He died a long time ago. Before she was born, even."

I touched her hand. "I'm sorry, Ms. DiBartola. I didn't mean to bring up a sensitive subject."

Lucinda's eyes narrowed. "Why did you come here asking about the dead man? We didn't know him."

I took a deep breath. "It's about the money. There were—"

"What's going on here?" A tall, thin man with thick gray brows over brown eyes came up behind me. "What're you doing, bothering my lady here?"

"She came asking if we knew that man who was killed down in Palm Dunes, Eddie. They're trying to find who did it."

Eddie stared down at me. "Why would we know him? He

had nothing to do with us."

I blinked in the face of the obvious hostility. "There were checks—"

"You gotta leave. Honey, you go inside. I'll take care of this." Eddie gripped my elbow and hustled me down the sidewalk. I stumbled as we got to the curb.

"Get your hands off me. Stop." I shook him off. "What's the matter with you?"

"What's a matter me? You come around here stirring things up, making a big fuss, getting Lucinda upset. It's old news. Old and forgotten."

I stepped back. "Mr. Cortini, did you know Al Leone?"

He was silent, his eyes forbidding. "I know no one by that name."

I caught the nuance. "Not by that name. But you know him."

Eddie looked away. "A long time ago, and you're bringing up bad things."

"Mr. Cortini, Lucinda's daughter Antonia—was Al her father?"

"What?" He squinted at me. "No! Antonia's father died long ago." He laid a hand across his chest. "God rest his soul. He was my good friend. That's why I take care of Lucinda now—because Antony was my best friend."

"Look, Mr. Cortini." I drew myself up as tall as I could stand, trying to look imposing if not intimidating. "Al's children know about the money going to Lucinda. They're trying to figure it out, and it's not going to take long before the police put it all together, too. You should tell me now, so I can explain everything."

Eddie ran a hand over his balding head. "It's so long ago. . .best forgotten. But there's the money. And I always knew that would cause trouble." He sighed, heavily. "Come sit here. I'm an old man, and I can't stand up to keep talking."

We moved to a green wooden bench nearby. I walked and Eddie shuffled. When we were settled, I turned to him, one eyebrow raised, waiting.

"A long time ago, we were boys together. Alec, Antony and Eddie. We came up in the old neighborhood, and in those days, the Family was very powerful. We thought we were bullet-proof, right? Alec and me, we were ladies men, a different girl every Friday night. But for Antony, it was always Lucinda. They got married, and she was just starting with a baby when we were asked to do a job. When you got asked, it didn't mean you could turn them down. No, you did it. Or else. I got very sick at the last minute, didn't go. But Alec and Antony went. They were fighting, the two of them, because Antony had promised Lucinda he was getting out and they'd move away. Alec didn't want him to go. But that night, things went bad. They went wrong. There was trouble, and at the end of it, Antony was shot. Alec said it was his fault, because he didn't protect him. And they were distracted by arguing with each other."

I could see it now, the story unfolding before me. "Alec. That was Al, wasn't it?"

Eddie nodded. "He was destroyed. He couldn't work anymore. He ran away, changed his name. We didn't know where, we never saw him again. But he promised Lucinda before he left that he would always take care of her and the baby. So the checks came, and they came every month for over fifty years."

"Did you know he was down here, so close to you?"

"No, not until recently. Then a friend of mine told me he knew someone who needed to ask a question about the Family. About something that might or might not be going on down here. I met up with the man, and it was Alec. We were both shocked. But I talked to him, and it was good. I told him, he had done good, making a life all these years and always remembering Lucinda. I told him, it was okay. That I was taking care of Lucinda now, and he could stop."

I licked my lips and looked hard at Eddie. "Did you shoot him? That night at Leone's, did you go back there and shoot him?"

Eddie paled. "As God is my witness, no. Jesus, Mary and Joseph, how could I do such a thing? Never. I had no reason to do it."

I believed him. This man and Al. . .both had taken care of their dead friend's family, for much longer than anyone could've expected. But what if someone else didn't see it that way?

"Mr. Cortini, who else did you tell? About Al. About where he was, who he really was?"

Eddie looked away. "I shouldn't have. I didn't mean to. But Antonia was here. She was visiting her mama. And. . .Lucinda was at bingo when I came home, and I was emotional. And maybe a little less for the wine." Guilt colored his face. "I let out the secret. I never should've said it."

We sat in silence on the bench. Seagulls cried overhead, and the breeze chilled me until I shivered.

"She shot him, didn't she?" I whispered the words, but I knew Eddie heard them.

"I don't have proof." Eddie covered his face with a gnarled hand. "I don't know. And I could never turn her in, do that to Lucinda. But when I heard what happened, I thought. . .yes, she could've. Coming up without a dad, no matter how hard I tried, it was hard on her. She's not a young woman anymore. She's old enough to be over it. But she isn't. I saw it in her eyes that night. She'd heard the stories, over and over, and in her mind, Alec was the one who came home when her dad didn't."

I took a deep breath. "Mr. Cortini, I have to tell Al's children. I don't know if there's proof, I don't know if there's anything the police will do. But I have to tell."

I expected him to argue with me, to yell or shout. But he only wagged his head.

"It was a long time ago. But he was a good man. He deserved more."

Chapter 13

"**S**O THAT WAS it. In the end, Al had done everything right, and that's what killed him."

I sat on the porch in my rocking chair, with Lucas on the step. It was Florida-chilly, meaning that the windows were open and the wind had picked up. I had a blanket around my shoulders.

"Yes, that pretty much sums it up. I told Dena the whole story, and they're turning everything over to the police. If Antonia doesn't confess, I'm not sure they have enough evidence to bring her to trial. Eddie won't testify. Lucinda has no clue about it, and she wouldn't say anything against her own daughter, either. Antonia's a lawyer who's rumored to be up for a seat on the district court soon. Who's going to believe she shot some old man down in Florida?"

Lucas reached for my hand. "Do you feel any better? Any closure?"

I sighed. "I don't know. I'm glad we have an answer. But at the same time, Lucas, it was because of me that Al called his friend, who sent Eddie to him. If I hadn't asked Al to do me a favor, Eddie never would've known that Al and Alec were the same man. He wouldn't have told Antonia. Does that mean Al's death is my fault?"

"Of course not. You might've asked the question, but everyone else along the way had a choice to make, ending with Antonia. She chose to pull the trigger. She alone is responsible, Jackie. Not you."

"I tried to tell myself that. I'm not sure I completely buy it. I let my imagination go wild, and that made me ask for the favor."

Lucas spread his hands in front of him. "If you're going to follow that route backward, then it's my fault for being a death broker and for moving down to Florida. And for not telling you right away who and what I am, so that you had to guess. And it's Veronica's fault for what she did to me. You've got to remember, too, Jackie, Al's end of life date was already set. I heard it the day I met him. It was his time. That should give you some little bit of comfort."

I nodded. "I guess. . .in a way, seeing you that night sending him on, that was my closure. I didn't know it at the time, but it was. It's what gives me peace."

"And you're giving him a legacy, too. At least part of it. In that cookbook, Al's spirit is going to be shared with people who never got the chance to know him. You'll pass on his philosophy and his food to the whole world."

"I'm working on it. We think with a little luck, we may be able to release the book before Christmas. I'm calling it *Food Like Heaven*. It's something Al said once."

"Al's children are going to love it. You should be proud of yourself." He kissed my fingers.

"I am." I hesitated. "Lucas, when I talked to Dena yesterday, she asked me if I might be interested in buying the diner."

I felt his surprise. "Seriously? What did you say?"

"I told her I had to talk to my boyfriend first." I smiled down at him. "It's a big decision."

"I can't think of anyone better to carry on Al's work there. But what would it mean for your column?"

"I don't know. But I've been thinking of making a change lately. I'm restless. I love what I do, but it's become so. . .rote. I'm not the kind of writer I always dreamed of being. And then I think of giving up cooking to become a full-time writer, and it makes my heart hurt."

"They're both part of you, Jackie. Two sides of your coin. Why should you have to do one without the other?"

"Yeah, you're right. But maybe I'm tired of cooking other people's dishes. I want to share my own recipes. I want to see people eat my food and rave about it. Does that make sense?"

"It does, absolutely. Have you looked at the numbers? Can you swing it? I'd be happy to help. I don't have much, but I'd buy in."

I smiled in the darkness. "Thank you. That's very sweet. But no, I think I can handle it. Dena said they're happy to hold the note for me, so I won't have to go out and get a loan. They just want to see Leone's live on. Another part of a great man."

Lucas tugged on my hand until I slid from the rocking chair and onto his lap. "Sounds like my girlfriend is about to become a restaurant owner. And a cookbook author. Is there anything you can't do?" He turned my chin, and holding my face with his fingers, he kissed me, deep and sweet.

"It sounds scary."

"I think some of the most worthwhile ventures in life are the scariest. I mean, falling in love with the guy next door who turned out to be a death broker and half-vamp was frightening, right?"

My heart beat picked up speed. "Who said I was falling love with that death broker half-vamp dude? Maybe I'm just using his hot body for amazing sex."

Lucas laughed. "And I'm perfectly okay with that. But I hope you *are* falling in love with that dude, because I know for sure he's deep in love with the crazy writer-chef who dashed half-dressed into his yard, fell right into his bushes and stole his heart."

I tilted my head to kiss him again, trailing my fingertips down his throat. "Love's a scary thing. I wouldn't want to do it by myself."

"You'll never have to. I'll be right by your side the whole time." He slipped his arms around me. "For the rest of time, and then some."

"We don't know yet whether you're immortal," I reminded him. I thought of Veronica, the mystery woman who had changed his life. She was still out there, a nebulous creature with murky motives. "There are still so many answers we don't have."

"The answers will come in time. I'm sure of it. And it doesn't matter whether or not life is everlasting when love is."

Lucas kissed me again, and I knew he was my everlasting.

The End

Epilogue

Veronica

I STOOD IN the shadows, just out of sight. I was near enough to hear their words, but then again, I'd have been able to hear them anyway. Incredibly good ears are part of the vampire package.

He held her in his arms, and I listened to the words of promise he spoke. I closed my eyes, sighing. The woman had been an unexpected complication. My seer hadn't predicted her involvement and couldn't see her future even now. I would've happily disposed of her, or perhaps even allowed their infatuation to run its course, but she troubled me enough that I hadn't yet made a move. Lucas lusted for her blood nearly as much as her body, and he couldn't hear her lifespan. I didn't know why, and I'm not a woman who tolerates mystery. I like to know.

As it stood now, there was time. I could afford the luxury of waiting. Soon, that wouldn't be the case. I needed Lucas. He had a role to play, and at some point I'd have to separate him from the mortal girl he fancied he loved. With a mumbled curse, I rubbed my temples. I didn't like complications any more than I liked mysteries.

The breeze stirred, and I breathed deep, taking in the scents of the two people cuddled on the porch. Tonight, I'd let them live. I'd slip away into the night without either of them guessing I'd been so close. One day, I'd have to act. One day, he'd have to choose. But this was not that day.

For now, they were safe.

Author Love

Thanks for reading *Death Fricassee!* If you enjoyed it, the absolute best way to show an author love and appreciation is to leave a review on at least one vendor site and/or Goodreads. I hope you'll do that.

If you'd like to chat books, come visit my website (http://tawdrakandle.com), my Facebook page (https://www.facebook.com/AuthorTawdraKandle) and Twitter (@tawdra). If you can't remember any of those, just Google me; as far as I've been able to tell, I'm the only Tawdra out there.

I do have other books out there just waiting to be read. If you enjoy paranormal romance and you liked the characters in this book, check out The King Series (it's Young Adult) and The Serendipity Duet (New Adult). Also, remember that *Stardust on the Sea* is the short story that tells how Lucas and Cathryn met in Cape May, before *Death Fricassee* begins. If sweet and sultry (non-paranormal) love stories are your thing, you might enjoy The Perfect Dish Duo (New Adult) and The One Trilogy (New Adult) or *The Posse* (adult). All these books are available in the usual hangouts.

And if you fell in love with Jackie and Lucas, book 2 will be out in 2015.

Playlist

Welcome to Mystery The Plain White T's
Breaking Anberlin
Under Control Parachute
For the Longest Time Billy Joel
Death and All His Friends Coldplay
Only the Good Die Young Billy Joel
Just Breathe Pearl Jam
The Night is Still Young Billy Joel

Acknowledgments

In 2009, when I had finished *Fearless* and was working on *Breathless*, I was part of a critique group called A Writer's Block. We grew large enough to need two groups, and since I was leading, I felt I should participate in both of them. For that I needed a secondary story. At this point, I was only writing young adult, but a persistent idea had taken hold in my mind, and it was not YA.

At this time, there was a flood of teen vampire/werewolf/shifter romance books in the market. They were great (well, at least most were), but I was not a teen, and I began to wonder, what if the girl who met the vampire wasn't a fresh and dewy young thing? What if she were older, more experienced and mature? And what if the vamp weren't a perpetually-20-year-old hot guy, but a man who'd been turned later in life?

And so Jackie and Lucas were born. Because I scaled back to just one critique group after publishing *Fearless*, I didn't finish their book at that time, but I always planned to do it after I finished The King Series. However, one thing and another happened. . .and Lucas and Jackie kept getting pushed back.

What was fascinating, though, was that while they waited, more of their story evolved. I realized this was not just one book, but entire series (how many books is yet to be determined). I also learned that Jackie and Lucas existed in the same world as The King Series. And so when I wrote a short story for the anthology *Eternal Summer*, with Cathryn Whitmore from The King Series as the female lead, I wasn't too surprised that Lucas was her love interest. How that all worked together has been seriously cool.

If you haven't read The King Series or The Serendipity Duet, you can always go back and enjoy more of Cathryn, Rafe and Nell in those books. And if you want to read about how Lucas and Cathryn met, the short story *Stardust on the Sea* is now available as a stand-alone book.

As always, huge thanks to my fabulous team of supporters: Mandie Stevens, who always wanted this book to be written and is always my biggest cheerleader; Amanda Long, who tells me the truth even when I really don't want to know it, makes my website pretty-pretty, designs kicking logos, gives sage advice and keeps me from making a fool of myself when I don't know what something means; Stacey Blake, who makes all of my stories so pretty and exhibits saintly patience with changes; Stephanie Nelson, who made this amazing cover, exactly what I wanted even though I couldn't articulate it and all my fellow Romantic Edge Books ladies, who inspire me daily and graciously give help and advice.

Huge gratitude and thanks to Heather Batchelder, for my gorgeous new author photos. (Flip to the back now and check it out. Go ahead. I'll wait.)

My readers make me smile every day. I love the funny and/or deep posts, the cheer-me-on messages, the reviews, the posts and tweets. . .you truly do rock my socks.

And of course, thank you to my family for extraordinary patience. This book was finished in the midst of a move that dragged out much longer than was planned, and I was often on the laptop while everyone else unpacked and organized around me. I appreciate the understanding.

Last but not least, thanks and love to my sister Robyn, who has been discussing this book with me for a long time and who gave me the character of Nichelle. Inspiration is everywhere.

About the Author

Tawdra Kandle writes romance, in just about all its forms. She loves unlikely pairings, strong women, sexy guys, hot love scenes and just enough conflict to make it interesting. Her books run from YA paranormal romance (THE KING SERIES), through NA paranormal and contemporary romance (THE SERENDIPITY DUET, PERFECT DISH DUO, THE ONE TRILOGY) to adult contemporary and paramystery romance (CRYSTAL COVE BOOKS and RECIPE FOR DEATH SERIES). She lives in central Florida with a husband, kids, sweet pup and too many cats. And yeah, she rocks purple hair.

Printed in the USA
CPSIA information can be obtained
at www.ICGtesting.com
JSHW031714140824
68134JS00038B/3685